To Eve ♡
Adrian
God Bless!
♡. Kayla ♡

THE LABEL DOESN'T
DEFINE YOU

KAYLA ROSE WARNER

THE LABEL DOESN'T
DEFINE YOU

Using Mental Illness for God's Glory

TATE PUBLISHING
AND ENTERPRISES, LLC

This book is designed to provide accurate and authoritative information with regard to the subject matter covered. This information is given with the understanding that neither the author nor Tate Publishing, LLC is engaged in rendering legal, professional advice. Since the details of your situation are fact dependent, you should additionally seek the services of a competent professional.

The opinions expressed by the author are not necessarily those of Tate Publishing, LLC.

Published by Tate Publishing & Enterprises, LLC
127 E. Trade Center Terrace | Mustang, Oklahoma 73064 USA
1.888.361.9473 | www.tatepublishing.com

Tate Publishing is committed to excellence in the publishing industry. The company reflects the philosophy established by the founders, based on Psalm 68:11,
"The Lord gave the word and great was the company of those who published it."

Published in the United States of America

ISBN: 978-1-68142-305-0
1. Biography & Autobiography / Personal Memoirs
2. Biography & Autobiography / Medical
15.02.23

I dedicate this book to God, that He may use it in any way that may bring people closer to Him.

Acknowledgements

Thank you to Jeremy for always loving me relentlessly. I love you, and I am so happy we get to walk this journey of life together. Thank you, Levi and Miles, for letting me write about you, with hopes that our experiences can help someone who needs encouragement. Thank you, Mom and Dad, for always being there during the good times and the bad, and supporting me in the writing of this book. Thank you to Janey, for always being so patient and forgiving. Thank you for proofreading the book and helping me with editing. Thank you to my dear brother and sister in Christ, Raja, and Kumari. You have inspired me more than you know. I am forever thankful to God for bringing us together and look forward to us all being together eternally. Thank you to all my dear friends who have been a support system for me over the years. I could write pages about how much you all mean to me. I love you all so much!

Thank you to Tate Publishing for making this book into a reality.

But above all, thank you, Jesus! Thank you for saving me, giving me hope and a story to tell. May You be glorified in everything, now and forevermore!

Contents

Prologue

It was the summer before my sophomore year of college. What a gorgeous day in the mountains! A group of us from our church's young adults' group had taken a weekend trip to a friend's farm in Montana. The sun was out, and it was a perfect day for a hike. We piled into the musty van and headed for the hills. My friend Brandy and I, our hair in pigtails, snapped a picture before heading up the trail.

We had some adventurous guys with us who decided it would be fun to climb up the side of the hill rather than take the marked path. Of course, I was adventurous too. Well, not usually, but today I was. Brandy and I began climbing up. The guys had headed up before us and were out of sight. A few minutes passed, and we began to hear yelling from above. Dirt and pebbles began crumbling down the hillside, then larger stones and rocks. Then, to my horror, a large rock began hurling down. It made a beeline for Brandy, striking her on the top of the head. I was two feet away, frozen in shock, as she tumbled down the distance we had previously scaled. The less daring friends below began the emergency calls. Soon, a helicopter from the nearest hospital swooped in and airlifted her away.

I felt nothing. Just numb. Something I never understood. Little did I know, this event would change the course of my entire life.

Introduction

I was raised in the church from infancy. God saw fit to bless me with two wonderful, faithful parents and I am so thankful for that. When I think of all the situations that I could have been born into, I realize that God has blessed me in countless ways. In some ways, I feel so guilty to be given so much when others have so little, many without any way to better their lot in life. But with great blessing comes great responsibility. I strongly believe that we are blessed in life in order to have the ability and resources to bless others who are less fortunate than we are.

When you are young, you don't really think about that sort of thing. I never really did anyway. Sure, I was thankful for my blessings, but it seemed like everyone in my corner of the world lived just like me. It wasn't until the last few years that I have realized the shocking reality that there is a world out there that doesn't know God.

That there are people who are hurting, people searching for the answers to the void they feel. There are people who live day to day, literally praying the prayer, "Give us today our daily bread." (Matthew 6:11, NIV)

This book is my faith journey. I will be sharing with you how my life has led me to the point I am at today in my walk with the Lord. God has shown me the truth in "For my thoughts are not your thoughts, neither are your ways my ways," declares the Lord. "As the heavens are higher than the earth, so are my ways higher than your ways and my thoughts higher than your thoughts" (Isaiah 55:8–9, NIV), and in "There is a way that appears to be right, but in the end it leads to death." (Proverbs 14:12, NIV)

My prayer is that you will be encouraged by my words. I had big plans for my life, but God turned those upside down. I want to share my story with you. I pray that if you have been, or are going through similar trials, that you will see that there is hope and peace. That there really is a light at the end of the tunnel, and it is found in the one who is light Himself. God revealed to me later the promise of "And we know that in all things God works for the good of those who love him, who have been called according to his purpose." (Romans 8:28, NIV) As they say, hindsight is 20/20.

Growing Up,
Practice Makes Perfect

God has always been in my life. Ever since I entered this world, I have been part of a family who loves the Lord and always makes being involved in the church a number one priority. I had a happy childhood, never lacking for anything. We were always well-off and had a lot of fun times together.

I was born in Yakima, Washington, on August 23, 1976. My family lived just outside of Yakima in a little town called Selah. Our house was surrounded by the apple orchard my grandpa and grandma owned. They lived just across the way, only part of the orchard separated our houses, and there was a path we would travel maybe a quarter mile to get to my grandparents' house. I first learned to swim in their large inground pool with a big blue curved slide. I happily look back on those memories.

I don't really remember anything specific before the age of five or so, and I know that age only because of videotapes I have seen. My brother was born almost two weeks before I turned five. I remember the VCR tape of me dancing around with Kermit the frog and the Miss Piggy dolls that my aunt had crochet for me as a "big sister" present.

The next memory I have is when my grandma was at home with hospice care. I was about seven years old at the time. I remember sitting by her and being sad that she was so sick. She had ovarian cancer. It was good that she could be home with us in her last days. I so look forward to seeing her again someday in heaven. My aunt says she wanted to be my guardian angel after she passed. The last memory I vividly remember was the day I woke up from sleeping in the special canopy bed, where I usually slept when I went to stay the night at grandma and grandpa's house. I walked into the dining room and saw my parents and my grandpa sitting around the table when they told me that Grandma had passed away. I don't remember anything more after that, except for a vague memory of seeing her in the casket for a moment at her memorial service.

I was always a very sensitive child. I worried a lot about things in general. But I wanted to follow God more than anything. One April night after I had been in bed for awhile, I began to feel afraid. I was terrified of going to hell, and I decided I wanted to be baptized right then. I came downstairs and talked with my parents. They agreed that I understood. I knew baptism was a huge and very important step in a Christian's life. It is the point at which we identify with Jesus in his death, burial, and resurrection. It is where our sins are washed away, and we are given a new life in Christ. God works within us to cleanse us from our sin.

It seemed as if my life began the summer I turned eleven. That summer, I joined the Selah Dolphins Swim Team. I wasn't much for team sports. I remember trying basketball, and it just wasn't my thing. So my parents thought swimming may be good, since it's more of an individual sport. The first race that I remember was at the Wapato Washington city pool. That pool was huge— fifty meters! I had to swim the butterfly stroke all the way to the end. I tried so hard. And then at the end, I was disqualified! This pretty much means all the hard work I just put in didn't even count for anything. Chalk it up to a learning experience. I'm pretty sure I never got disqualified in the butterfly again!

Despite that "false start" (pun intended), that summer was a lot of fun. I even got the Most Improved Swimmer for that year! Since I enjoyed swimming so much (and I wasn't too bad at it), I joined the YMCA year-round swim team. The part I despised was going to practice. Once I got there and in the water, I was fine. But sometimes, it was like pulling teeth to get me out of the house! (Just ask my dad and he will tell you plenty of stories). The worst thing was when I started going to early morning practices for about two hours before school. I remember countless days of getting ready for school after practices, attempting to massage the goggle rings from around my eyes. Then sometimes, I would have to do doubles, which meant back to the pool after school!

One of my coaches always wanted me to set goals for myself. Well, I wasn't really interested much in setting goals for swimming or "visualizing" myself winning and setting records. God was always first, and I never let swimming come close to competing with Him for top priority. It was sometimes hard to juggle out-of-town swim meets with attending Sunday morning worship at a Church of Christ in the area. My mom was so good about making sure we all stayed on track and kept our minds on God. I am so thankful to her for that.

My dad was my biggest fan. I still remember him driving me to practice at five in the morning and then sitting outside the pool at the viewing window, watching me practice. Sometimes I think he was more dedicated to it than I was! I am so thankful that I have a dad who always cared so much about me. That really made an impression on me.

But oh, how I hated to practice! I remember locking myself in the bathroom one day after school, refusing to go! And that was almost the extent of my teenage rebellion. Wow, so childish, but I really didn't want to go. That made a point I guess, because my dad still tends to remind me of that incident from time to time. The thing is, I always felt so much better after I went and was always glad I did when it was said and done. But if I never practiced, would I have gotten any better at swimming? Of course not!

On a side note, I can see how "practice" relates to my spiritual life as well. Sometimes I would just avoid studying God's word because I felt like I had to do other things. The truth was, I wanted to do other things. But if I got into God's word on a regular basis, especially a daily basis, and also wrote in my prayer journal, I always felt better. If I never read the Word of God, I won't grow as a Christian. I will remain in the current state I am, and that is an unhealthy place for a child of God to be in. I also need to study in order to share the hope I have with others. If I don't see the joy in my life from being a Christian, I certainly won't be sharing it with anyone else! They won't want what I have because I won't look any different from the rest of the world.

There have been many times I have just had to ask God to give me the desire to be in the Word. I had to be honest with Him (He knows what I feel anyway), and the truth was I wasn't too excited about studying. I didn't have a motivation. And when I have prayed this prayer, which has usually been when I wasn't very consistent with my prayer journal, I might add, God has always given me a spark of interest in something biblical, whether it be a book, sermon series, or Bible study that gets me back into His Word again.

School Years

I was the model A student and the overachiever. Typical of the firstborn. We are talking about the girl who cried about getting an A- in high school because it ruined her GPA. I have a report card where a student teacher commented that "Kayla is the most organized fifth grader I have ever seen." Thus the perfectionist conundrum of my life began.

We moved from Selah, Washington, to Richland, Washington, after my sixth grade year. I was so sad to leave my friends, especially the cute, blonde-haired, blue-eyed boy I was "going with" at the time. However, my grandpa and my step-grandma still lived in Selah. Being that we were only an hour and a half away, we could all keep in touch pretty regularly.

I joined the Tri-City Channel Cats team right away. Once the coach started to see my potential, he had me to really focus on the breaststroke. The two hundred and one hundred meter became my best events. I qualified and went to the Junior Olympics when I was fourteen years old! Of course, right after that is when we decided to move back to Selah because of my dad's job. I never did quite get back to those fast times again. I guess different coaches have their own styles, and I missed my old coach and his workouts. I occasionally wonder, *What if we would have stayed in Tri-Cities, and I kept training like I had been?* But I knew in my heart even back then that becoming an Olympic swimmer was not God's plan for my life. Not to mention it wasn't ever really a plan I had for my life either.

I started back to school at Selah High and got in touch with the friends I had left in sixth grade (yes, including getting back together with blonde-haired blue-eyed boy). I was excited to begin high school, especially being on the school team. I was able to be on a relay that went to state and then in two individual events—the one-hundred-yard breaststroke and five-hundred-yard freestyle. I swam to sixth place during my freshman and sophomore years at state in the breaststroke.

Then we got this crazy idea to spend the summer before my junior year in the Tri-Cities in our motor home so my brother and I could swim for the Channel Cats. I missed my coach and never did very well since I left. So for the love of swimming, we hooked our motor home up to the side of our church building, which was around the corner from the city pool where we practiced every morning and afternoon. We even showered at the pool. It was like camping out all summer. Obviously, swimming had taken over our life for some time by now, but this was borderline nuts! But I will say it was fun.

That summer was amazing. I had not worked so hard in who knows how long, and it felt great! I didn't make my Junior Olympic time again, but I came really close to it. Instead, I went to the Inland Empire Zone championship in Mission Viejo, California. This was a blast, with a bunch of people from teams we always competed with from surrounding states coming together as one team for the meet.

At least it was a blast until I got sick. Really sick. I mean, throwing up, flulike sick. None other than on the day of my main event, the two-hundred-meter breaststroke. Yes, the one I had been training for *all summer*. One of my roommates also got sick. It happened to be the day of her best event too! I struggled through the prelims, just making the last slot in the final. I really didn't want to swim it. I was so bummed! It was like all my hard work went down the drain. *Why?* Why get sick *now?*

So it came down to final time, and I hadn't really been able to keep much down at all. So my energy was pretty much zilch. My grandpa had made his famous spaghetti sauce and sent it over with my grandma, who came to watch me swim. I remember sitting in our motor home, chowing down on spaghetti. I was feeling much better.

I got in the water to warm up before my event. I felt pretty good. The worst thing was, I was on the outside lane, with the wall on one side. The middle lanes were always best. I remember getting ready to go up to the blocks, not looking forward to swimming this again, after feeling so awful earlier that morning. So up I stepped onto the diving block, and the starter said, "Take your mark." The shrill beep signaled the start of the race. Diving in, my goggles instantly began to leak. They fogged up. Now that's just great. Okay, I just had to get through it. Now if I could see the wall, it would be nice. I heard my coach yell, "Go," at every breath. I actually felt pretty good in the water and just kept going for the four lengths of fifty meters. And then I reached the end. I did a two-hand touch, came up, and heard a lot of screaming. I turned around to see my time…I had come in first place! I could not believe it! My time was barely a second slower than my personal best. I just started praising God then and there, praying prayers of thanks all during the cool down in the practice pool. It was amazing. I felt amazing. I had also swam a meet record and made the top sixteen for the event. That moment meant even more to me than actually making the Junior Olympics. I remember it so vividly, how fast I felt gliding through the water. But there was something else that happened. Remember my roommate, the one who also had the flu? Well, she repeated history right after me! She also won her event and set a meet record! At the awards ceremony for our team, besides our

The Label Doesn't Define You

medals, we each received a paper plate that had "Hint Number One: Puke First" written on it. I still have it. Everyone got a great kick out of that!

Well, after all that, my family decided to move back to the Tri-Cities. There were more opportunities for my swimming, especially for the high school, and I could train with my favorite coach. It seemed like the perfect plan. But all our best laid plans don't always fit into God's plan.

I hated my new high school. I missed my friends in Selah. Swimming for the school team was torture for me. We did dry land training on top of swimming, and I dreaded practice even more than ever. Think of running up and down the high school football stadium bleachers and then swimming in the pool for two hours. All this was outdoors until the end of October. I felt like all I ever did was go to school, go to practice, do homework, sleep, and do it all over again!

My parents made me a deal. If I got through the high school swim season at the end of the quarter, then I could begin to homeschool. My mom was already homeschooling my brother and sister. So that is what I did. With God's help I made it through the state meet. I placed eighth at state in the one-hundred-yard breaststroke. I was at an AAA school now instead of an AA. Plus, everyone was a little faster. I was not too happy when I saw I could have gotten second or third in AA!

I quit swimming altogether after high school season that year. I was seventeen years old. So that is my life from five to seventeen in a nutshell. All in all, swimming kept me in great shape (and out of trouble) through my growing up years. It also kept our whole family constantly busy. Swimming year-round is a very consuming sport, and it takes over your life.

I remember writing a letter to my year-round coach about why I was quitting. It was long and drawn out from what I recall. I know a lot of it had to do with explaining that God was most important to me, and that I wanted to focus on Him more, and not swimming. I don't know if he ever understood that, since he was not a religious person. But he definitely knew that I was! I did end up doing a little coaching for the team a few months before I left for college, which was fun. But apart from that, I didn't do much swimming anymore. I do still love it and like to teach lessons and go with my kids to the health club now. Maybe one day I'll join a master's group to just keep in shape. As I look back, I think God protected my sanity through those years of swimming. If it wasn't for that, my illness may have been triggered considerably sooner than it was. So despite the occasional misery, I am thankful to God and my parents for getting me involved in swimming.

I was so relieved to be able to stay home and continue schooling. I had my friends in the church, so I didn't lack the social aspect, and we were also part of a homeschool group who met once a week. It was accredited so I was able to graduate in June of 1995 with an officially recognized diploma. I also went to a skills center my senior year and studied dental assisting. I received Most Employable Student both semesters. It was unfortunate that I never did get a job as an assistant. Mostly because I was planning to head to college out of state that fall.

So here we are at the next chapter in my life—post swimming. After I quit, I had the dilemma of how to stay in shape. I had never had to watch my weight before with all the swimming I was doing. I could eat donuts and pizza every day if I wanted to (and sometimes I did just that!). I was petrified of gaining weight! To me, it would be the worst thing in the world. I had the idea that I just *had* to stay skinny. If I didn't, I feared I would never find a husband. And I just knew if I ever gained weight after I got married, I'd never hear the end of it.

I became so obsessed that I began working out every day with a friend. We would stay in the weight room at the gym for close to two hours every night. I stayed in shape, but not without stressing about it. I got into the habit of pressing on my stomach constantly. It got to be where I'd do it without even being aware of it.

My senior year, I became very strict on my eating. I would have the same things to eat all the time. I remember having thin sliced deli ham and cutting out as much of the marbled fat that I could.

My obsession with the fear of weight gain even got to the point that I binged really bad a few times. I felt so mad at myself for losing control that I purged several times. The only problem was that I made myself gag and throw up so hard that it broke blood vessels in my eyes. I couldn't hide that, and my parents guessed what was going on right away. They told me if I didn't snap out of it, I wouldn't be going away to college that fall. Well, that was the motivation I needed to stop being so obsessed. I really wanted to go to Cascade, a small Christian college in Portland, Oregon.

Cascade was previously Columbia Christian College, and it was where my parents met. It was a dream of mine to go there and find the love of my life, just like my mom did. I had it all planned out: I would go to school and take general education classes toward a career in dental hygiene, since I had already taken dental assisting my senior year. I wanted to be a dental hygienist because I knew it would have a flexible schedule, perfect for being a mom. My secret motive (and a popular joke among the guys at college) was that I was going for my MRS degree. Well, I wasn't about to ruin my chances for that! There weren't many options in the Tri-Cities at the moment.

I am naturally quiet and introverted. But I really didn't want to be that way. I had made up my mind to be an extrovert in college. I wanted to get to know everyone on campus and in the meantime scope out Mr. Right, of course. Granted, the campus wasn't very big, only about three hundred, but you get the idea.

I never had a serious boyfriend before. My mind just wasn't focused on that too much in school, besides a few crushes here and there. My freshman and sophomore years in high school, I was a little boy crazy, but what girl isn't at that age? The guys I liked were more of a platonic relationship. Nothing physical. I knew I wouldn't get serious with any of them. I had my ideals that I wanted in a husband, and for him to be a devoted Christian was at the top of the list.

I never really kissed anyone until college. What played a big part of my fear of any physical relationship was of course God and also an event that happened in seventh grade. I had a crush on a boy in my band class. I decided

I was going to kiss him. So we met in the band room after school one day. I gave him a peck on the lips (which surprised him) and then we both ran our separate ways. I still remember he had been drinking root beer! It's funny, the things that stick in our memories. Of course, my best friend told her mom, who told my mom. I don't remember any specifics about what my parents said, but I do know I felt extremely guilty and sinful. After that, I was scared to death of kissing anyone!

In ninth grade, I called a boy I liked a few times, and because I disobeyed my parents who thought it was "too forward" for a girl to call a boy, I was grounded from going to church camp. Yes, that's right. I guess that was the only thing my parents knew I cared about enough to make an impression. It worked. Thinking back, I'm pretty sure that was God's way of protecting my emotions from running wild. So I avoided serious relationships throughout high school and just hung out with the single young adults' group in our church. And after the fairytale dream I had of marrying my handsome workout partner from church fell through, I was ready to leave for college. I was ready to spread my wings and fly!

Hypocrite

I loved everything about my year at Cascade College. It was like one big long party! I am amazed that my GPA for the first semester was a 4.0, and the second, only one B kept me from having a straight A college record.

It didn't take me long to find someone to date. My first boyfriend was a guy who was studying to become an orthodontist. Perfect! This is *the one*. He just had to be Mr. Right! And he wasn't too bad on the eyes either.

He was my first kiss. I remember it was on the playground at the Christian school next to the college campus. We were sitting on the slide. Of course, I had told him I'd never been kissed. I'm quite embarrassed to say what he said after kissing me the first time. Would you believe that he told me that I kissed like a dead fish? How he knew what it was like to kiss a dead fish, I'll never know. I don't know why I didn't smack him upside the head and run when I had the chance! No, I took that as a challenge to prove him wrong!

That's when I started to be a hypocrite. The sad thing is, I didn't even realize that's what I was doing until much later. You know, the hindsight's 20/20 once again.

I was such a good "church girl." I was (technically) faithful. I never missed a Sunday morning, evening, Wednesday night service, or Bible study. I even got irritated at that boyfriend of mine if he missed Bible class or church.

But every night that we could, we would sneak off and hide around the campus's make out spots. Now some of you may be thinking, *What's the big deal? There's nothing wrong with that.* But let me tell you, it was a big deal for me. I take the Scripture very seriously when it says, "If anyone, then, knows the good they ought to do and doesn't do it, it is sin for them" (James 4:17, NIV). I just couldn't honestly say that Jesus would look at us and give us an applause for what we are doing. So I put God away in His little box and took Him out when it was convenient for me to do so.

The excitement wore off after a while, and the guy broke up with me right after we returned from our first school break. I wanted to be with him any time I could, and he still had a bunch of friends he liked hanging out with so I lost that contest. But whenever he wanted to kiss, I was a real sucker. I must have changed his opinion from our first kiss because he never got tired of leading me on.

It took me forever to get over him. In fact, I almost made the biggest mistake of my life with him when I went to stay overnight at his parent's house when he gave me a ride back to school after Christmas break. Thank God that He was there to keep me from making a bad choice that could have impacted my entire life. However, the fear of my parent's wrath was more prevalent than God's disapproval at that point. But that night still makes me shudder when I think of what could have happened had I not listened to the Holy Spirit whom I had been ignoring all this time.

The rest of the school year flew by. One of the interesting things that happened was getting back in contact with that boyfriend I had in sixth grade off and on throughout my freshman and sophomore year. You remember, right? The blonde-haired blue-eyed one? He had gone into the air force right after high school. It so happened his grandmother lived just a few blocks from Cascade. He and I had started dating again, long distance.

When he came on a break to visit, I was so excited to see him for the first time in about three years. But there was no chemistry whatsoever. I really had hoped there would be! He kissed me for the first time that night, as we sat watching a movie at his grandma's house. Then he popped the question right there. He said he didn't have the ring yet, but he wanted to ask me. We had talked some about marriage in casual phone conversations, but I really wasn't prepared for him to ask me to marry him on the first night we had seen each other. So I told him it was too soon, and that was the end of it. I hadn't planned to be a military wife. Plus, he wasn't a strong Christian. Frankly, he just scared me off. After I broke it off, I didn't hear from him for a long time. I vaguely remember hearing something about him getting married, but I haven't heard from him still to this day. I sometimes wonder where his life took him. I hope he is happy and has found someone to love him as deeply as I know he loved me.

I had a relationship on the rebound, and after doing other things I regretted, summer came. I ended up breaking up with him during the break. I was especially feeling guilty for my behavior throughout the school year with boyfriends. I vowed that the next year, I would stay more focused spiritually. I even wrote a letter to be opened by my future husband on our wedding night, in which I vowed that I was saving myself for only him.

I had gained about twenty pounds over the school year (that cafeteria food with desserts at every meal did me in). I faithfully began walking off that weight and by the end of the summer was back to my precollege size 5. I was feeling great! Things were working out just right. I was optimistic for what the new school year would hold.

Until the accident.

Falling Apart

It was the summer before my sophomore year of college. What a gorgeous day in the mountains! A group of us from our church's young adults' group had taken a weekend trip to a friend's farm in Montana. The sun was out, and it was a perfect day for a hike. We piled into the musty van and headed for the hills. My friend Brandy and I, our hair in pigtails, snapped a picture before heading up the trail.

We had some adventurous guys with us who decided it would be fun to climb up the side of the hill rather than take the marked path. Of course, I was adventurous too. Well, not usually, but today I was. Brandy and I began climbing up. The guys had headed up before us and were out of sight. A few minutes passed, and we began to hear yelling from above. Dirt and pebbles began crumbling down the hillside, then larger stones and rocks. Then, to my horror, a large rock began hurling down. It made a beeline for Brandy, striking her on the top of the head. I was two feet away, frozen in shock, as she tumbled down the distance we had previously scaled. The less daring friends below began the emergency calls. Soon a helicopter from the nearest hospital swooped in and airlifted her away.

I felt nothing. Just numb. Something I never understood. Little did I know, this event would change the course of my entire life.

Praise God that Brandy miraculously survived that accident. She suffered no brain damage or any other side effects. God definitely had a plan. However at the time, I didn't realize it included me.

Because I was a resident assistant, I was required to be at the college a week early for freshman orientation. One of my main duties included being in charge of checking the rooms each night at curfew to make sure everyone was safe and sound. One of the perks was having a room all to myself.

Brandy came to visit me that week of orientation. She had her eye on one of the up and coming freshmen. She was able to camp out with me in my room for a few days. Being with her again after her recovery from the accident triggered something inside of me. I think I finally felt the emotion and the significance of what had happened that day. As Brandy and I talked, she told me how God must have a plan for her life to allow her to survive the horrible ordeal. She was searching to find her purpose.

It really didn't occur to me until then. It could have been me that was struck by the rock that day. The guilt of how I'd been living my life came rushing in, consuming me. What if it had been me? What if I had died that day? Would I have gone to heaven? These questions plagued me for several days and nights.

The events of that accident in a way reflected how I had been living my life over the past year. I had strayed from the path God had set before me. Instead of following the road that I knew would take me safely to my destination, I chose to do it my way—to go against the clearly marked trail. It looked to be adventurous and exciting! Forget that boring old trail. Instead of trusting God's way was best, I was telling Him my way was better. And isn't that what sin really is? God tells us the way He knows is best for us, and we choose our own path. It's like we are telling God, "I don't trust You. My way is better." It dates all the way back to Adam and Eve. But if we're honest with ourselves, don't we all eventually learn (some more painfully than others) that God's way is always best? I'm inclined to believe so.

By climbing up that mountain on my own, I thought I wasn't completely turning away from God. I mean, wasn't I heading in the same direction? I had found a better way to climb! Sure it was harder to climb up than to follow the path, but I needed to show myself and other people that I could do it.

This is like thinking I need to prove to God that I love Him by doing something. I am striving so hard to repay Him for what He did for me through Jesus. Wasn't it just too easy, even simple, to follow the path of grace He has laid out before me? If anything seems too good to be true, it probably is, right? Didn't I have to do something to earn His approval? I had to "work out" my salvation with fear and trembling, didn't I?

Looking back, I see God was teaching me the lesson of His grace. Yet it has taken me until just recently to even begin to understand. I never will completely get it, but I'm getting closer.

It's amazing what God allows to happen to draw us closer to Him. Sometimes it takes a lot of pain and suffering for someone to really understand that the path they are taking doesn't have to be so hard. I was trying to work my way back to God. With the weight of guilt, I was beating myself up about my sin. But Jesus died so I wouldn't have to. This was the lesson I needed to learn.

During those days that Brandy spent with me, I began questioning my salvation. *Am I right with God?* I wondered. I knew I had accepted Christ as the Son of God and had been baptized for the forgiveness of my sins at the age of eleven, but did I really understand what sin was? Surely not as I understood it now. The confusion of not knowing and not being confident in my salvation began to take its toll.

When Brandy left and school began, I had a lot on my plate. On top of the resident assistant job, which kept me up late every night, I was taking some tough classes that were prerequisites for dental hygiene. My classes included anatomy and physiology at Warner Pacific in Portland. Cascade didn't offer that class, so I had to borrow a friend's car to drive over there.

On the first day, I sat in class as we began going over the syllabus. When the teacher mentioned we would be dissecting Maude, a human cadaver, my stomach turned. I became nauseous as I got a visual picture in my head. Anxiety set in. No, I would *not* be doing that! I decided then and there I was going to drop that class as fast as you would pull your hand off a hot stove!

I remember that after leaving Warner Pacific College, I got lost on the way home. My mind was clouded. I was overwhelmed. This would change everything! What if I couldn't be a dental hygienist now? I had to take anatomy and physiology, and there wasn't anywhere else I could take it that I knew of. Did I really want to be a dental hygienist anyway? Why did I even want to do that in the first place? I didn't know anymore. I called my friend who had loaned me her car from a restaurant pay phone. I was so upset that I think she may have even come to pick me up. It's kind of a blur.

Getting right on task of dropping that horrendous class, I spoke to a counselor about switching my major to education. Sure, I could be a teacher. They got the summers off to be with their kids and could be home when they came home from school, right? That seemed a lot less stressful.

Also, a boyfriend I had met at church camp in seventh grade and I had recently gotten back in touch and started dating. He had just begun his first year at Cascade. He was a wonderful Christian, someone I could see myself marrying. That took the pressure off for finding Mr. Right.

But adding to the stress was the fact that he ended up being roommates with the "first kiss" guy from freshman year. The relationship that I was beating myself up about over and over again. It was quite uncomfortable for him as well! It's all a little jumbled in my head as to when exactly, but around that stressful time, I just up and broke it off with the supposed man of my dreams. I don't remember the logic in that, but at that time, I probably wasn't concerned about logical reasoning. I'm sure he would have been able to help me through this if I had just opened up to him.

But the final breaking point was in church that next Sunday morning. I was sitting between a friend and another guy I had recently met. It was during communion. All I remember is right in the middle of it my mind clouded over. I felt all numb, and I ran out crying. I know a friend came in to see what was wrong, but I can't tell you who it was for sure. I remember I couldn't even talk. I had a major mental breakdown right then and there.

It was at that point that I decided I wanted to leave college and move back home. Well, I didn't really want to leave, but I knew I had to. Something was wrong. Very, very wrong. I didn't understand what was happening to me, and I didn't want anyone asking me about it. It was terrifying.

I knew that at the root of it, there was a spiritual battle going on in my mind, struggling with doubts about my salvation. Flashbacks from the accident that summer, stress of school and my impulsive breakup with my boyfriend all played a part. Everything had been perfect. Now everything had fallen apart in just a few short days.

Calling and talking to my dad was very hard for me to do. He was so disappointed about my decision. But he hadn't been there nor felt what I was going through. My mom came and picked me up, and I moved back home.

I can only imagine what rumors began circulating around the college. One of the girls asked if I was pregnant as I was packing up. Thank God it wasn't that on top of everything else! I had dodged that life-changer. Thanks to Him and my parents.

My dad's condition was that if I came home, I had to enroll at Columbia Basin College there in town. I agreed. And I tried. But I had begun to have a social phobia of crowds. I just couldn't handle it. I didn't know anyone in my classes, and I felt completely alone. I did have some friends from my church attending CBC, but I didn't see them around much. In desperation, I quit going to college. I realized I couldn't function normally anymore. I needed help.

Downhill Spiral

My mom took me to see a counselor. I remember I hated going. I felt hopeless. I would never get married, have a family, or a career. My dreams were gone. I felt like I had no purpose for living whatsoever. I'm sure some of you reading this have felt this way at one time or another, so you will relate to this deep, dark feeling of despair. My mind was racing; I couldn't get it to shut off. And the anxiety was constantly looming. The counselor started me on an antidepressant.

I found out that my family had a significant history of mental illness. There was major depression and manic depression (or bipolar disorder) from both of my grandparents on my mother's side. With my first counselor, the possibility of me having manic depression was discussed briefly. However, for an official diagnosis

I would have to have a full blown manic episode. The closest to mania could have been my year at college when I consistently had high energy and was obsessed with boyfriends. But I had never had a real manic episode like the counselor described. So for now, bipolar was on the back burner. I remember we tried different types of medications (and cocktails as we call it when we have several medications), but nothing seemed to help.

Classic to depression, all my thoughts centered on me. It is a very selfish disease. Satan uses it to keep us so focused on ourselves that we lose focus of what really matters in life. The first step is submitting to God, and the next is to tell Satan to flee. God promises he will, in James 4:7. My mom would always tell me to get outside of myself and do things for other people, but it really did help to focus on someone else other than myself. That's what love is all about. It took me a lot of intentional (sometimes forced) good deeds before I began to default to this way of thinking. I have to remind myself from time to time, but once it's practiced enough, you feel much better and useful in the kingdom of God, even in the midst of your struggle.

I remember that I never turned my back on God. But I was scared to death of Him. I pictured Him with an angry look on His face, condemning me to hell. I played games in my mind. If —— happens, then I'm okay, and if not, I'm going to hell if I die right now. It sounds strange, but some of you may know what I mean. I was in continuous torment.

I remember my mom trying to encourage me with a few hymns we would sing in worship. "When We All

Get to Heaven" and "Because He Lives" are two of the most meaningful songs for me during that time in my life. Even thinking of those songs just now brings tears to my eyes.

Because I was so paranoid about my salvation, I studied with our minister and decided to be rebaptized. I knew that the doubts of my salvation were a big part of my breakdown, so maybe this would help ease my mind. I was so excited and wanted to tell everyone about the Gospel. I was on a spiritual high for about a week. Maybe it was a little situational mania. You would think I was through with feeling condemned after this, but I still had a legalistic mindset that I had to be doing things for God, to earn His forgiveness. I felt worthless, and I just knew God was mad at me. I felt like if I didn't get things all figured out, I would still be lost. I had absolutely no understanding of grace. I read the book *In the Grip of Grace* by Max Lucado, which helped somewhat. But for some reason, I felt like it was too good to be true, and I must be an exception. It wasn't long until I was back to the pit of despair.

All I wanted to do now was lay around, eat, and sleep. I avoided any friends who tried to reach out to me. Especially Brandy. That twenty pounds I had worked so hard to lose over the summer came back on quickly, and I couldn't have cared less. I'd grab a carton of Maple Nut ice cream and eat the whole thing. There wasn't any reason to care. I wasn't suicidal yet, but I was getting close. My nightmare was just beginning.

I vividly remember one day being in my parents' bedroom. I was staring at my dog Kaytie. Voices in my head were condemning me. I wanted them to stop. I remember thinking I must be demon-possessed. I did the only thing my mind told me would help: I screamed at the top of my lungs. After the screaming, my parents decided I needed more help than they could give me. At this point, I'm sure I had mentioned that I wished I was dead.

They took me into the counseling center and checked me into the inpatient unit most commonly known as the mental ward. I was scared. The people there were crazy, and now I was one of them. I was terrified of dying, but I couldn't take living any more.

It was a safe place, well-staffed, so I couldn't hurt myself although I did try to. I pressed brush bristles into my arm during a visit with my parents. I tried to eat some water color paints that I had brought. I ran out to tell the staff after I did and found out they were nontoxic. I was afraid of shaving with my razor, because I feared I would cut myself on an impulse. I told them so then I could not have a razor. I was placed on suicide watch.

For inpatient, there are different "levels." The most restrictive was suicide watch, where you had to stay out in the common area, could not leave for any activities, or go to the lunch room. They brought the food back to the commons area. If you went in your room, the door had to stay open, and they would check on you often. On levels 1, 2, 3, and 4, you were given more privileges the higher the level. You earned a level based on participation in groups, therapy, setting goals, the psychiatrist's and counselor's recommendations. Level changes could be requested at the end of the day. At the highest level of 4, you were able to leave with family for a few hours so they could see how you did out in the community. After being at this level and seeing how we did on extended visits, we would be discharged. You could also go down in levels depending on your behavior.

We saw the psychiatrist daily. They managed our medicines and changed the doses as needed. The hospital was the quickest and safest way to get on and off medications because they could watch you and monitor you every day for any negative reactions, side effects, or improvements. Although the daily 6:00 a.m. disruption of nurses taking my pulse and blood pressure was quite annoying, the longer I was there, the better I felt. I began to see the benefit of being there.

If I remember correctly, I was there at least two to three weeks that first stay. When I went home, I wouldn't say I felt like myself again by any means, but I was somewhat better. My mind wasn't constantly racing, things were somewhat better controlled. But it would be several years until I felt like my old self again. At least, what I could remember of who I used to be.

Besides being confusing to my younger brother and sister, I think the whole situation was most difficult for my mom. She had a great job in ad sales for our local paper that she had got to help pay for my college tuition. But she had to take quite a bit of time off because I was so codependent. Being closer to my mom than anyone, she was my "safe place." I felt like as long as I was with her, nothing bad would happen.

But I couldn't be around her all the time, so we found some wonderful people in our church whom I would go stay with during the days when she was at work. I would alternate between staying with different people. One lady let me come stay with her during the day at her business. I helped an elementary teacher as a volunteer in her classroom for a while. I remember lying on one lady's couch, just staring at the ceiling, watching the time tick by.

I needed a schedule of things that I could do during the day to keep busy. Playing cards helped some, also watching *I Love Lucy*. It was most detrimental for me to just sit and think. My mind still raced and wouldn't shut off. I was on antipsychotic medicine, but it didn't do much for me. It was so humiliating, but there was absolutely nothing I could do. It was just how things were. I couldn't be alone. I didn't know what to do with myself.

My mom's boss was not very understanding of her taking time off to take care of me when this or that came up. She even advised her to just put me in an institution and let them deal with me. Things got so bad that she ended up just quitting her job because she felt like she needed to be home with me. But I don't remember really feeling bad about it. I was happy I could be with her all the time now.

I did eventually get to the point that I could handle taking a stress management class at CBC, which went well and was quite helpful. But I dropped the sociology class. I think it was because the teacher said she was an atheist, and I didn't want to hear her ideas. Religious things were still a very sensitive subject for me.

Having to drop out of school and classes was hard for me. I had always been a great student, very consistent and dependable. Now I was becoming someone who would just give up if things became difficult, or even if I just didn't like something. Yet another thing to be disappointed about.

At one point, I started feeling well enough that I begged my parents to let me go back to Cascade and try it again, with a light load. They let me go. However, it wasn't how I had dreamed it would be. I felt out of place, and people seemed to treat me differently. Plus, I wasn't the same way I used to be. I was pretty much the exact opposite. From what I remember, I wasn't too easy to get along with either. I ended up leaving again, which depressed me even more.

But God had a plan that was about to unfold. One that I never could have dreamed up. He was about to make good on the promise I had been clinging to for the past few years.

"And we know that in all things God works
for the good of those who love Him, who have
been called according to His purpose."

—Romans 8:28, NIV

Hope

On August 13, 1997, my dreams that had been put on hold began to come to fruition. It had been about a year since my breakdown with severe depression. I was beginning to have some more hope that things might get better. There was a light at the end of the tunnel, so to speak.

My family had a season pass to the local water park in town. My brother, sister, and I had been going quite often during the summer. That day, the youth group from the church we used to worship with in Yakima came down for a day of fun in the sun. My good friend Ryan and some other friends were coming, so we met them there. I remember I wasn't feeling too well, and I even debated on leaving before they got there. But when they arrived, I quickly forgot about going home.

Ryan had brought two friends from school with him. All of them had just graduated in '96, the year after me. They were both pretty cute and I, of course, was available. I was putting some sunblock on Ryan's back when one of his friends, Jeremy, came over and asked if I could put some on him also. I said, "Hi, I'm Kayla. I'll be your masseuse for the day!" Oh my. I could not believe that had just come out of my mouth! What a pick-up line!

We did end up hanging out all day. He pretty much ditched his friends, and we went up and down the waterslides endless times. My little sister, Jenna, who was ten, tagged along with us most of the time too, but we didn't mind.

What impressed me right away was how open and honest he was with me about anything and everything. I felt completely comfortable with him. It was like we had known each other for years. You know, one of those kinds of friends where you just hit it off with right away.

At the end of the day, we exchanged phone numbers, and he had already made plans to come back to town in a few days so we could hang out some more. He still teases me now because my sister told him about our conversation in the car on the way home. I was telling my parents about this guy I'd met and how we spent the whole day together...and then I drew a blank. "Jenna, what was his name again?" I'll never live that one down!

I never forgot his name again! Because once we met, that was it. He would drive back and forth from Yakima to the Tri-Cities in between shifts at the nursing home where he had been working as a certified nursing assistant for several years. He was going to school at the community college to become a nurse.

Jeremy is the only person I have ever met who could survive and then drive on with so little sleep. Once he worked a double shift of sixteen hours, went home, and made chocolate chip cookies, then drove to the Tri-Cities. He called me on the phone and said, "Look out the window!" There he was with cookies and a huge stuffed animal for my twenty-first birthday! Then he drove right back home, took a nap, and then headed back to work! Now if that isn't being in love, I don't know what is! This was less than two weeks after we had met.

We mutually decided to remain friends for a month and see if we wanted to begin a more serious relationship after that. There was marriage talk toward the end of the month, and we had decided to give each other some sort of promise token. We shopped for our gifts together. We got all dressed up and went out to dinner at a fancy restaurant to "officially" begin what became our lifelong relationship. At dinner, he gave me a beautiful opal promise ring, and I gave him a watch that had "eternity" written on the face of it. It was a sweet beginning to our relationship, and we have pictures and fond memories of that night.

We were in agreement to wait to have sex until we were married. We even tried not to kiss…but that only lasted for about a month after we started dating. It was hard for us to draw the line for physical closeness after that, so we had to be careful to remind ourselves to use self-control. Once the physical aspect enters a relationship, it makes things much more difficult. Looking back, I wish we had waited to kiss until the day we got married, which was our original plan.

The Proposal

Jeremy is such a romantic! The way he asked me to marry him was so special. I will never forget it as long as I live.

I had taken a job as a CNA to get a feeling for what Jeremy did. I worked a night shift for about a month at an assisted living home. I had worked the previous night and was sleeping all day, for I had to work again that coming night shift. When I woke up that evening, my mom and dad told me we had to leave to go somewhere. Then they handed me a little card. I opened it to read, "Riddle me this, riddle me that, go to the place we first met at." So we headed for the water park. It was December and chilly out, but Jeremy's dad was standing there outside waiting to give me a rose, along with the next "clue." The scavenger hunt led me around to all the places where we had had our first dates: the gym, the mall, the restaurant where we had our official first date, and the gazebo in the park where we ate our leftovers the next day! There was a family member or friend waiting at each spot with a rose and the next clue. The last place I was told to go was "where we danced upon the waters." This was referring to where we had gone after our fancy restaurant date, out to a pier off the Columbia River.

It was December 13, 1997 and coincidentally the night of the city's annual Christmas Lighted Boat Parade. As I stepped onto the pier, Jeremy was stepping off a lighted boat, handing me a rose, and asking if I want to go on a boat ride. So we stepped on and climbed up to the top of the houseboat where Santa's sleigh sat. He got down on one knee in that little sled and asked me to marry him! There we were, in the middle of the Columbia River in a boat parade playing Mr. and Mrs. Claus! Of course you know I said yes.

We proceeded down below to visit with the owners and have some hot chocolate. I found out that the boat ride wasn't even planned! Just a little final touch by God Himself. The people who owned the boat had come over to the dock thinking Jeremy was a family member whom they were waiting to pick up. When they came by, Jeremy explained he was going to propose to his girlfriend and asked if they would mind if he took me up in the sleigh on their boat. They said yes, so that is how our fabulous engagement story came to be.

Wedding Plans

Originally, we planned for a June wedding. I say originally because we ended up getting married in February. Here is the story to how that happened.

Jeremy was driving back and forth and we had been engaged for close to two months. We were getting a little antsy to get married, if you know what I mean. I remember having an argument with my parents about something. I was twenty-one, so I felt I should have more freedom than what they were giving me. Yes, I had been very sick, but since I had met Jeremy, I had been doing pretty well.

It was evening. Jeremy had been visiting and was about to leave and head back to Yakima, so I decided to go with him. I just wanted to get away for a while, and Jeremy lived with his parents, so it wasn't like I was going to be completely alone with him at night. On an impulse, I snuck out from the upper deck of our loft, ran down the stairs, and left with Jeremy. He wasn't trying to get me to leave with him; it was all my idea. There was a horrible icy snowstorm that night, which made for quite a slick ride back to Yakima. I spent the night in Jeremy's older sister's room, since she was out of town that weekend.

The next morning, I talked with my mom. Needless to say, she was extremely upset! She said we should just get married or break up. Frustrated, she commented, "Valentine's Day is next week. Why don't you just do it then!" So I looked at Jeremy and told him what she said, and we decided that's just what we would do! Jeremy agreed, but I'm sure he felt pressured when I put him on the spot. So we had one week to plan the wedding!

I had already bought my dress with some money I earned working at the assisted living place, and we had already purchased the bridesmaid dresses. Our church building was available and so was the minister. Unfortunately, Ryan couldn't make it for the wedding. My parents paid for most of the wedding. Despite how irritated, I'm sure they were with me. I was thankful for their blessing. Other family members helped a lot with the preparations to make it a day to remember. Jeremy's aunt and uncle made arrangements for us to have a wonderful honeymoon in Leavenworth. Even a good friend from church, who was a professional cake decorator, made a beautiful cake for the reception as her gift to us. Even with the one week notice!

The way everything came together, it just seemed to be God's timing. We ended up having around two hundred people at the wedding, even though it was so last minute! The ceremony was beautiful. We were so happy, just two kids giddy in love. Many people from the three congregations I had attended growing up came, and a lot of friends and family were able to make it. Unfortunately, my grandparents weren't able get to there, being that they were in Arizona for the winter.

I'm pretty sure some people thought I was pregnant because of this wedding being so spur of the moment. But that wasn't the case. In fact, getting married sooner was to prevent that from happening! We had both promised God and each other we would wait until we were married. So that's what we did.

At the time I am typing this, we have been married for sixteen and a half years. Our last anniversary, we were reading through some old letters we had written each other by "snail mail." We didn't e-mail much yet back then. I had saved a whole box of letters from our dating times. We met in August 1997, were engaged in December, and married on February 14, 1998. Just six short months from meeting to marriage. Before we were married, we made the commitment to stay together no matter what. With God's help, we have had a wonderful marriage. Of course we've had our ups and downs, as you'll see in the pages ahead. But we have always kept God at the center of our relationship from the very beginning. I know having that mindset helped us. Going into a marriage putting God as the first priority and the determination to make it work has made all the difference for us. There were some really scary times that he could have left me, or I could have left him. But we never gave up on each other.

With God, all things are possible and His guidance through our trials makes us stronger. When we allow perseverance to finish its work in us, we mature in Christ.

> "Not only so, but we also glory in our sufferings, because we know that suffering produces perseverance; perseverance, character; and character, hope. And hope does not put us to shame, because God's love has been poured out into our hearts through the Holy Spirit, who has been given to us."

—Romans 5:3–5, NIV

6

Answers

Our married life began living with Jeremy's parents. At such a sudden shift in plans, that was the easiest most logical thing to do. Jeremy was now attending the two-year nursing program at Yakima Valley Community College, so I planned to just find a job as a CNA again in town. Our time at Jeremy's parent's house lasted one month. We were able to move into an apartment then and stayed for about six months. Then the lady next door to Jeremy's mom and dad decided she would rent her house out to us for under $300 per month so we moved into the cute little red one-bedroom house. We fixed it up with some new carpet and made a few other improvements. It was perfect for the two of us.

Then the depression began to hit me again gradually over the first year of our marriage. The honeymoon was over, so to speak. I couldn't keep a job. I would want to be with Jeremy when he was at work, so I would go there when he was on night shift once in a while. I was clingy, hated being alone, and was not motivated to do anything. My relationship with Jeremy's family was rocky, and I resisted any help they would offer. I remember letting the dirty laundry pile up so high and Jeremy's mom coming over and asking if she could help. I would be so angry because I felt like by doing this, she was pointing out what a horrible wife I was. I sadly remember having a lot of resentment for her. One day, Jeremy and I were sitting in the living room, and we must have forgotten to turn the burner on the stove off because a fire started. I just looked over and saw it and mentioned nonchalantly that "oh, the stove's on fire," and just sat there as Jeremy got up to put it out. I seemed to just not care about anything. My medications weren't helping either, so it seemed. I began going to counseling again and trying some different medicines.

We decided that I would be better off if I had the support of my family in the Tri-Cities. Jeremy was reluctant to agree but reasoned he could transfer from YVCC to the CBC nursing program. The only hang-up was that he had to pass a test to waive taking an extra class that was a requirement at CBC. He had to do this before he would be accepted as a transfer student. Jeremy took the test but wasn't able to pass it. There would not be a spot for him until the next school year, provided that he took the class or the test again.

When this happened, we had already moved there. Jeremy became so discouraged that he gave up on nursing completely. He got a sales job at Future Shop electronics store. Since I was feeling a little better with my family close by, I got a job as a housekeeper and nanny for three kids.

So what do people usually do when they have two incomes? Spend money. We went out and bought a brand-new Kia Sephia, with a whopping $300 a month payment (which was pretty expensive back in 1999). Why that car? Jeremy liked the name. Plus, I was going to have to drive these kids to school and back, so I needed a dependable car, right? Buying the car proved to be a big, expensive mistake.

It was a real struggle for us as a married couple, and it got even more difficult in the months to come. Future Shop went out of business. Then I found out I was pregnant.

It got very hard to do my nanny/housekeeping job with all the nausea and morning sickness due to my pregnancy. The parents of the kids I was taking care of were kind enough to let Jeremy help me out, since he had lost his job. So that worked for a while. One thing is for sure, God always took care of us, no matter what. The money was always there when we needed it, be it by miracle, generous family, or friends.

A few months later, Jeremy landed a job in the school district as a sub-custodian. He had some pretty regular work, getting some long-term subbing jobs. We were able to get an insurance. We were also on State Medical, and later WIC benefits, because of our income and me being pregnant, so that was a great blessing. I ended up quitting the nanny job after Jeremy got the sub job. The morning sickness was really more like all-day-especially-in-the-car sickness.

I had heard (or convinced myself that I had heard) my counselor say that I could wean off my medications while I was pregnant. It sounded good to me! They weren't really helping anyway. So gradually, I went off them, convincing myself they weren't good for the baby.

At the beginning of the school year, I applied for a position as a head dive coach for an area high school. Don't ask me why. I didn't know anything about diving! My expertise was in swimming. However, they really needed someone, and the man who had been the head coach for years wanted to retire. He agreed to train me and stay on as an assistant at practices. The season started at the end of August and concluded with state in mid-November. But I didn't end up making it through the whole season. In October, the mania began.

An extreme episode of bipolar mania is hard to understand if you've never experienced it. But I'm sure some of you readers will know exactly what I mean. In some ways, it's a blur as I look back. But I'm sure my family remembers.

Just because of being pregnant, my hormones were going pretty wacky. But on top of that, my moods were more extreme due to being unmedicated. Besides coaching the dive team, I was teaching swimming lessons and early morning water aerobics classes at the gym. I began to get less and less sleep. I was superenergized. I argued with people and talked nonstop. Jeremy said I would switch from topic to topic so fast that he couldn't keep up or get a word in edgewise. I thought I knew everything and was always trying to figure things out and read into meanings of what people would say. Paranoia set in. I believed people were out to get me. I got a tape recorder and decided I was going to record conversations so I would have proof. Anyone who knew me growing up or now could tell you this was not like me. But I thought I was just fine. In fact, I had never felt better! I felt such clarity of mind, creativity, and ambition. I could do anything! I once went to early morning practice to work out with the swim team when I was seven months pregnant. I have a video that Jeremy took of me swimming where I'm talking about me going to the Olympics that year in the breaststroke. I was very serious, like it was a matter of fact. I remember reasoning with my "logic" that I would just bring the baby in his carrier beside the pool while I practiced every day!

About that time, I had to go on some medication to help slow down contractions. I had a lot of preterm labor. Go figure! I could probably count ten times that I went into the hospital thinking something was wrong. I remember reading that this medicine had a side effect of triggering mania. That didn't help matters one bit.

I'm sure you would have guessed that Jeremy and I were not getting along. I was getting virtually no sleep at night. Maybe a few hours tops. But I felt just fine. My mind was constantly racing, thinking, coming up with grandiose ideas and plans. I would get angry at the most insignificant things. I would impulsively throw objects and once even smacked Jeremy as hard as I could on his back. I remember him running out the door and down the sidewalk of our busy street, as I ran after him, screaming at him that I was sorry. My poor, sweet, and enduring husband, I honestly don't know how he lived with me.

Because of all the interpersonal relationship problems I was having, the athletics director at the school had to ask me to step down from my coaching position due to "complications from my pregnancy."

The final straw was the car. Jeremy's birthday was coming up the next month. At the time, we had two cars, the Kia and Jeremy's Mazda he had from when we first met. Jeremy had mentioned this certain car he really liked at a sports car dealership in town. I got this fantastic idea that I was going to surprise him and trade in his Mazda for that sweet sports car. However, when I got there, Jeremy's bright yellow dream car wasn't there. But there was a white Chrysler Sebring with a black automatic convertible top.

I had been dressing quite provocatively, especially as a pregnant woman. I was wearing short skin-tight dresses and a lot more makeup than usual. I got all dressed up and marched myself right down to the dealership and told them I wanted to buy that car. I don't even remember how much it was, but I'd "figured out" that we could definitely afford the $400 plus payment (on top of the $300 Kia). The interest rate was over 20 percent! I somehow convinced the dealers we could afford it. Then they told me I had to have Jeremy's signature to finalize the deal. They let me drive the convertible over to where he was working and bring him back there to sign the paperwork. Jeremy was quite shocked when I drove up and "surprised" him. I told him, right in front of the salesmen, that if he didn't sign the papers, I would divorce him. Backed into a corner, Jeremy signed for the car. Jeremy had to work a little longer, so he went back to work, and I went and picked up a friend. We drove around, got some food, and then I went back to pick Jeremy up from work after his shift.

Once my parents found out about what had happened, they tried to convince Jeremy that I needed help. He wasn't really on board; however, my parents were insistent. They kind of tricked me into going to a crisis response center. I would have never gone on my own. I was just fine! My parents had to hire a lawyer to convince the dealership to void the sale of the car due to my mental instability.

I became an inpatient at the same behavioral health center I had stayed at when I first had my breakdown. But this time, I was admitted involuntarily, meaning I couldn't leave until they agreed I was okay to go home again. Here I am, almost eight months pregnant, sleeping on an uncomfortable, twin-sized, hard mattress, and I have a roommate. And did I mention I was extremely angry at everyone?

I remember taking out my little phone book (yes, the good old days before everyone had a cell phone) and making calls to a lot of people. I know I must have sounded crazy to anyone I talked to. I was explaining why I shouldn't be there and how everything was not fair and how angry I was at my family for tricking me. One of the staff nurses was constantly on me about me being on the phone so much. She gave me a limit of one fifteen-minute phone call per hour. I remember being so mad at her! I also tried to make myself go into labor so I could leave and go to the hospital. They ended up taking me over to get me examined one time, only to send me right back because I was just fine. I was there at the counseling center as an inpatient for about three weeks. After my release, I was assigned a case manager and home health nurse and was on a kind of probation at home that was to follow me for several months after our baby was born.

Although I was miserable at the time, it was also the best thing that could have happened to me. As I look back, I can see that God was using all things for good. Because of having this manic episode, I could finally be officially diagnosed with bipolar disorder. They were then able to give me Lithium, the strongest, oldest, and most dependable drug used for stabilizing mania in bipolar patients. Within the three weeks of my hospital stay, the Lithium, along with some other meds, balanced me out considerably well. With this medication, lab work has to be done to monitor the amount of Lithium in your blood. There needs to be just enough to be therapeutic, but not too much or I could become toxic. Once my levels were on target, I felt more like myself than I had for a long time. Praise God! I thank Him for what happened. I wouldn't want to go through it again, but I wouldn't ever trade it for what I learned. I feel bad for all the people who had to put up with my ranting and raving and strange behavior. I am also thankful that the damage done to my relationships was repairable, because unfortunately, for some people in these situations, that is not the case. After I was feeling more stable, I even began to enjoy a great relationship with my mother-in-law. When things were all said and done, I realized that everything worked together for good. I was finally able to get on the right medication.

7

Tough Beginnings

I was thirty-eight weeks pregnant. I had just plopped down on the mattress in our bedroom floor to talk with an old friend from my college days. It was Jeremy's birthday, and we had just returned with his mom and dad from dinner at Red Lobster. Earlier that day, I had made a Ding Dong cake, a favorite of our family. We were leaving soon to go over to my parent's house to have cake with them.

As I finished up the phone call, I pulled myself up off the bed, and as I did, *woosh!* My water broke! I ran to the bathroom and told Jeremy we needed to go to the hospital because my water broke. He didn't believe me! I guess I'd cried wolf too many times. When I showed him how much water there was everywhere, he was convinced. We headed for the hospital, with the cake in tow.

Jeremy already shared his birthday with a cousin, so he was joking that he didn't want to share it again. I guess Levi respected his wishes from the womb as he arrived at 12:37 a.m. on November 21, 1999, so they each have their own special day and don't have to share. But we all know how it ends up going when family birthdays are close together—celebration compilation!

Levi looked to be a healthy baby boy, and things were looking good until a few hours went by. Jeremy was watching him when he thought he saw something like a seizure happening. He called the nurse over, and they informed the doctor that something was wrong. After some observation, it was determined that he was also having trouble breathing. His doctor feared that he may have a heart problem.

There was not a hospital in town that could deal with infant heart problems, so he was placed in an incubator and immediately airlifted by emergency helicopter to Sacred Heart Hospital in Spokane, Washington. Jeremy was able to accompany him, but I had to stay. I was told I could not leave the hospital until I had been there for at least twenty-four hours. Besides that, my epidural hadn't even worn off yet. I had to wait until the next day to go to Spokane.

How scary it was to have a baby and then see him shipped off right away! Plus my husband wasn't there with me either. But thankfully, he was able to be with Levi. The situation was completely out of my hands. But my comfort was that Levi was being held in God's hands. And I was forced to trust that.

When I was able to be discharged the next day, my parents drove me to Spokane. Jeremy and I stayed in a hotel next to the hospital as they took care of Levi in the Neonatal Infant Care Unit (NICU). Praise God that he did not have a heart problem! We were told he had bronchopulmonary dysplasia, which is a fancy way of saying that his lungs were not fully developed. He was on oxygen in a tent, and we could not even hold him for the first few days of his life. We had to don scrubs and wash our hands meticulously before we could even enter the NICU.

On Thanksgiving Day, Jeremy and I decided that morning that we were going to pray and fast for Levi. We asked God if He would please allow us to hold him that day. We prayed in faith that Levi would be doing well enough that he could be out of the oxygen tent. I'm not sure how long we prayed, but whenever we left to go over to the hospital and walked into the room, God had answered our prayer! Truly, it was a day of thanksgiving! We walked onto the unit, and the nurse asked us if we wanted to hold our precious baby boy! And there he was, no oxygen tent, just a nasal cannula. We have never forgotten the power God showed us following that time of intense prayer and fasting. It was a great faith builder that God gave us in His perfect timing.

Levi continued to get stronger, and after ten days, he was allowed to come home on oxygen with the nasal cannula and a strict regimen of steroids. Levi developed asthma, and we had many trips to the hospital during his first few years of life. When the nebulizer medicine, steamed up bathroom, or cold night air failed, it was off to the emergency room in the middle of the night for a dose of steroids. There is no feeling more helpless than those of a parent who can do nothing to make a child feel better. A common cold became the precursor for croup and asthma attacks.

We moved out of our upstairs apartment and temporarily moved in with my parents so they could help us take care of Levi for the first month after he was home from the hospital. Then we settled in at a double wide in a mobile home park not too far from my mom and dad's. It was a nice place, and we enjoyed having a place that was bigger and comfortable. Plus lots of storage space!

Jeremy had a permanent custodial position in the school district by this time, so we had dependable income, and I was able to stay at home with Levi. When Levi was three, we noticed that we could build a house, and our mortgage payment would be just about the same amount as we were paying for our mobile home with lot rental. So we found a lot out in West Pasco. At the time, it was out in the middle of nowhere, with only a gas station and a McDonalds nearby. What more do you need, right?

We built the smallest floor plan, just over 1,000 square feet, with three bedrooms and two baths. It was just right for the three of us. Jeremy's parents helped us with the down payment and landscaping costs. It was fun and memorable to have a house built; we even put up the fence ourselves along with my in-laws. We have lots of pictures from start to finish. It's great to look back and reminisce.

Speaking of reminiscing, I have a little story to tell about Levi. It was the week after we moved into our new house. We were awakened by a little boy running into our room, crying, covered from head to toe in what looked like chocolate. Jeremy sprang out of bed and noticed little brown footprints leading to the kitchen. "Kayla! Get the camera!" Jeremy shouted. I complied and came in to find a lovely mess of cocoa powder, smeared all over the floor with a little apple juice mixed in! There was some pepper sitting there too.

Levi was saying he was trying to make chocolate milk. I think he must have rubbed pepper in his eyes. I scooped him up and put him in the bathtub, pajamas and all. "Mommy, I'm having a chocolate bath!" Levi smiled. All we could do was laugh. We knew it would be a great story to tell someday. The footprints even came out easily with a little hot water.

Son after My Own Mind

Levi was a sweet little boy, the light of our lives. But around four years old, we began to notice some significant problems in his behavior. He was going to Pre-K at a private Christian school, and soon after the school year began, we started getting phone calls. He was doing strange things like wiping his nose and spitting on his desk and then licking it and other people. He wasn't fitting in socially. He didn't have many friends. He wouldn't lie down and be quiet at nap time and would disrupt the whole class. So much that they called and asked me to come in and lie down with him at nap time and try to keep him quiet! I only went once, but it gave me an idea of his social behavior.

In our church, we were constantly feeling like everyone else's kids were perfect, or at least it seemed that way. They would sit still throughout the worship services, where Levi was the exact opposite. He would even get kicked out of children's church. Think about having a kid who answers aloud when the preacher asks a question during a sermon. Not to be funny, but because he actually thought he was supposed to answer. However, he wasn't learning from his mistakes. It was like things weren't getting through to him.

Disciplining him was a nightmare. It was like nothing worked for very long. It was hard to be consistent in parenting when he would adapt to whatever we tried so much that it was no longer effective. On occasion, we took out all the toys in his room, just leaving his books. He still entertained himself and didn't seem bothered in the least to lose his toys. It was frustrating to find things that worked, and then he would end up repeating the same things over and over, so we never knew if he really learned from a punishment.

We didn't have a clue what was going on. Our minister's wife, who was a special education teacher, approached me one Sunday. She mentioned that she saw traits in Levi that her older son exhibited when he was younger. Her son was diagnosed with Asperger's syndrome, a type of high functioning autism. She suggested I read a book by Tony Atwood *Asperger's Syndrome: A Guide for Parents and Professionals* and then see what I thought. Ten years ago, I had never even heard of that, so I'm sure not too many other people had either.

I read the book, and it sounded exactly like Levi! There was an evaluation you could do at the end of the book, and when I filled it out with Levi's symptoms in mind, it was very evident that something like this was going on.

Besides one of the main symptoms of Asperger's social awkwardness, he had a problem with loud noises. Levi hated the happy birthday song. We aren't quite sure what triggered that, but possibly a birthday cake toy he had seen that moved and sang happy birthday was the culprit. He also hated any talking toy or stuffed animal. The song always triggered a complete meltdown. Any time it was sung, to him or anyone else, he would cry, scream uncontrollably, and cover his ears. Imagine your child having a birthday party, but not being able to sing happy birthday. Or when we were somewhere, like at a restaurant, and they come out singing a birthday song to someone's table. This once happened at Red Robin, and he cried and hid under the table. This type of reaction went on for years. Thankfully, when he was around ten or eleven, he learned to cope with it.

After we noticed all these things might indeed add up to something, we took him to a doctor who specialized in autism. We did testing in the forms of questionnaires for Jeremy and I and Levi's teachers and an observation done by the doctor. She diagnosed him with Asperger's syndrome and sensory dysfunction at four years and eight months old.

Now, if you know anything about Asperger's, these kids are pretty much little geniuses—socially awkward but impressively smart. They tend to fixate on one or two subjects that are of interest to them and then learn everything about them. Levi's obsession was with trains.

We had bought a video called The Alphabet Train, which he watched over and over again. He learned so much about them that he could talk your ear off! He was like a walking encyclopedia. At two and a half, he knew his alphabet and how to spell his name. He preferred to converse with adults rather than kids his own age. Any adult who talked with him for even a short length of time commented to us about how intelligent he was. He always articulated his speech very well and used big words for someone his age. Sometimes we would get bored with his constant talking, but he never ceased to amaze us with how smart he was. In third grade, his IQ testing scored near genius levels in the area of building and design, which fits him, as he now spends nearly every waking moment either building things out of Legos, playing Minecraft, or reading.

Before his official diagnosis, the school district would not give us any services to help him. We had him tested several times, but because he was so smart, they dismissed any disability. He doesn't look any different than any other kid, but to see any difference in typical behavior, you would have to spend more than an hour with him in a social situation. People didn't know much about autism back then. In the last ten years, it has become a big subject with all the statistics going up. I read recently 1 in 68 children are affected worldwide. When Levi was born, it was 1 in 110.

It was very hard for Jeremy to accept this about Levi. Of course, all dads have big dreams for their kids. Not that moms don't, but with dads and boys, it's different. The fact that Levi was socially awkward and not interested in sports was hard for Jeremy. We tried T-Ball, but that just resulted in him zoning out into his own world when he was in the outfield. Sometimes the coach would ask me to help keep him on task. Of course, for Jeremy, this was embarrassing. It took a while for him to accept Levi's diagnosis. One fear he had was that Levi may never grow up to live on his own. Jeremy didn't want Levi in special education because he feared he would be labeled for the rest of his life. He didn't oppose getting the diagnosis but knew once the school was involved, we'd never get him out of special education. But then there is a choice to make. Do you help your child learn the tools he can use to succeed in life or deny a problem and watch them struggle through? We decided to give him the best environment for his learning and see how it went.

Once his diagnosis was in place, we were able to get him on an individualized education plan (IEP). He was able to attend an autism social skills kindergarten class in the morning and a general education class in the afternoon to practice the skills he was learning. We created picture charts at home of the activities he did and had a routine we followed each morning that he checked off. He did best when things were structured.

I am confident that this early intervention helped him get to where he is today. We had to keep trusting God to take care of Levi and help him in his frustrations and meltdowns and making friends. I encourage any parents with a child who has an autism spectrum disorder to seek the earliest intervention possible. If you suspect something, get it checked out as soon as possible. Don't stay in denial. Lay aside your pride. The best thing to do is to equip your child for life. Look at things from the big picture of what is best for your child's future.

I would love to say "problem solved!" but that most definitely was not the case. As Levi got a little older, we discovered more unusual behaviors, behaviors that didn't quite fit in with autism. We thought his hyperactivity may be ADHD, but he really didn't have difficulty concentrating. It was mainly behavior problems. He began saying strange things and drawing disturbing pictures. He would just slip off into his own "Levi World," as he called it. Yet when he looked like he wasn't paying attention and you asked him a question, he could repeat verbatim what you had just said. He would bang his head on the mirror in the bathroom. In fact, he was doing that so often, and he would get so distracted in the bathroom that we took down the whole mirror. Levi would have extreme rage over something small that wouldn't bother most people, such as missing a problem on an assignment. At school, he would rip up his papers, throw pencils, and flip over chairs. At home, it was often triggered by telling him no. He would scream and hit at me. When he would get like this, I would just close his door and let him have at it— destroying his room. Then he would snap out of it, be all upset at himself, and want to punish himself for what he had done. He would say he wished he was dead. All of this was at six years old.

There were several times that we were really concerned about his safety. It really worried us when we found a large kitchen knife on the top bunk of his bed one morning. There were cut marks from the knife on the ceiling. We locked up the knives after that incident. One

Fourth of July, we weren't going to be out watching the fireworks because I needed to go to bed early on account of medications. I woke up about 12 a.m. and went to the kitchen for something to eat or drink, and I noticed the front door was unlocked. Then I saw a person walking around outside. I went over to the door, and it was Levi, walking around! I looked in the driveway and was surprised to see that Levi had a setup of a blanket, pillow, coloring books, crayons, and snacks. He decided to have his own little party. Some of the neighbors had seen him while they were out front watching the fireworks, came, and knocked on the door, but I hadn't answered. Maybe that was what woke me up. Jeremy wasn't home at the time. I think he was working a swing shift, and we expected him home fairly soon. I remember being thankful Jeremy didn't drive on home and up into the driveway when Levi was out by himself.

Of course, there were all the times at school that Levi got himself suspended for one reason or another. One time in grade school, he was mad at a girl and took a fruit bar out and a plastic knife and said, "This is you," and proceeded to saw the bar in half. That got him sent home for a few days. He had threatened to bring a knife to school and kill someone. We almost expected a call from the school at least once a week. Eventually, he was put on a behavior plan so he wouldn't get sent home every time he made an empty threat.

In the meantime, with all of this going on about Levi, I was beginning to have physical complications from the Lithium. It made me so thirsty that I was drinking literally gallons of water every day. I started becoming incontinent at night. Eventually, I began to have problems with that during the day also. I had also begun having manic symptoms again, which meant the Lithium must have been getting flushed out of my system. I remember staying up all hours of the night obsessively researching the differences between ADHD and pediatric bipolar disorder.

Jeremy and I decided it might be time for a medication change. I was afraid to change my meds slowly over time since I had responsibilities with Levi and was also working part-time. I didn't want to risk any problems. We spoke to my doctor, and he agreed that I could be inpatient while they got me off of the Lithium and onto another mood stabilizer. I had been on Lithium for six years, and it had worked so well, so I was a little nervous about switching medications. But being there at the hospital, they could watch me for side effects, be there during any withdrawal symptoms, and do the change quicker than I could have from outpatient therapy.

So for the third time, I was admitted to the hospital. The first time I saw my psychiatrist while I was there, he told me that at the rate I was going, if I had not gotten off the Lithium, I would have had kidney failure in two years. That really scared me! I was so thankful to get off of that medicine at the time I did. My new mood stabilizer was Lamictal, and it has worked well for me the past eight years.

When I came home, of course there was still the problem with Levi. We were able to get him in to see a psychiatrist. Within ten minutes of observing Levi, he gave him the diagnosis of bipolar, ADHD, and Asperger's.

He told us he does not usually diagnose a child with bipolar at so young but gestured to Levi, "How can I not?" Hearing this was a relief but also sadness. Relief to finally find out what else was going on and that we could do something to help him. Sadness in the fact he would have to deal with this all of his life too.

It is hard to decide for your child to be on medications, but the alternatives could be much worse in many cases. The true test would be if the medications helped him. They did! We saw a huge difference and so did his teachers. They said he was like a different kid! In Levi's case, as a child prone to self-injury, threatening to harm others and himself, we were willing to try whatever we could to keep him safe. If you had a child suffering from juvenile onset diabetes, the insulin would be crucial to the child's survival. With mental illnesses, the same is true. The chemicals in the brain need to stay balanced just as the insulin in the body needs to stay balanced. Some people just don't make the insulin, and some people don't make the chemicals to keep their mind balanced. I don't know why medication is resisted so much for mental illnesses but not for other bodily illnesses. Death can be imminent in both cases, though the mental aspect can be more subtle.

Over the years, Levi has had adjustments in his medicines, including a trip to the inpatient child ward at the behavioral health center at one point. We maintain a good relationship with his doctor that originally diagnosed him with bipolar. He now says Levi is like a completely different kid than when he came in that first day about eight years ago. He is very proud of how he has matured and learned to cope with his disorders.

As Levi has grown up, he has become a fine Christian young man. Jeremy and I both think that once he made the decision to follow Christ and be baptized that he finally got serious about his attitude and behaviors. At the third quarter of his eighth grade, he no longer qualified for an IEP, and no longer received special education services. The only thing we missed about that was the front door bussing we had since his kindergarten years! We are thrilled with his performance in the general education classes that last quarter when he pulled all A's. His intelligence was never the issue. It was the behavior problems that held him back. He was picked by a lottery system this year to go to a charter school here in town. He attends Delta High School, a Science, Technology, Engineering, and Math (STEM) school. This allows him to focus and excel in his talents and favorite subjects. It is also a smaller school, with a total of around four hundred kids. He has a 504 plan in place in case he needs any accommodations for test taking and some assignments if needed. This will follow him throughout his college years also. We see Levi as becoming a great asset to the community someday as an architect, engineer, or maybe even a rocket scientist. Praise God for how well he is doing now!

Smiley Miles

Jeremy decided to go back to school to become a nurse, as he had always wanted to do. He was just finishing up his prerequisites for the program. It was nice to see him decide that he wanted to do this and go for it. He was able to get into the program right after finishing due to doing an excellent job on the entrance exam.

When Levi was about seven, things were going better with him, and we had been debating on adopting another child. I had never considered even having another child myself because the medications I was taking had not been safe for a baby, especially in the early stages of pregnancy. And there was no way I was going to go off my meds again. I had learned my lesson the first time!

One time when Jeremy and I were both at an appointment, my psychiatrist mentioned that people have had children while taking the same medications that I was currently taking. When we heard this, we began thinking maybe we should have another child because it sounded like things would be all right if I continued taking my prescriptions during the pregnancy. We were excited because we had never thought we would ever have an opportunity to do this. We had originally wanted to have two children. After we decided this, I think it was the next month or two that I found out I was pregnant. How fun it was to tell Levi he was going to be a big brother! He was excited that he would have some company.

The pregnancy went really well. In fact, I had never felt better. I stayed on my meds the entire time and diligently prayed for the baby to be protected from anything that could harm him. I stayed active exercising, including doing water aerobics, throughout the entire pregnancy. At seven months, we hiked up Multnomah Falls and all the way around the mountain then back down. It was a little extreme for that late in the pregnancy, but I remember doing just fine.

The birth was virtually pain-free. I had an epidural early on, and another medication that I was regularly taking for anxiety was also used for nerve pain, so that is probably why I couldn't feel any pain. That was a nice perk!

There was a time when my blood pressure dropped very low, which was scary. No one told me how bad it was until they got it back up again by giving me a lot of fluid through my IV.

At around 7 p.m., I had asked the doctor if I should take my evening pills, stating they did make me quite tired. He said I could, so I decided to. Miles was born at

10:02 p.m., and he was very sluggish and would not take a breath right away.

Thankfully, we had decided to go to the hospital with the NICU this time around, just in case there were any problems. It ended up that Miles stayed there for several days. I was bottle-feeding due to the medications (as I had with Levi). He was having problems learning how to suck and swallow, so the nurses were working with him to get him to drink his formula. He was very slow at drinking, so it took a few days to get him up to the amount milk they thought he should have. We got to stay the last three or so nights with him, and the staff taught us how to coax him to drink as they monitored his intake.

I did have some postpartum depression with Miles and ended up going back into inpatient at the hospital again for a few days to adjust things. Since that hospitalization, I have been doing really well and have not had any major relapses. I work hard alongside my supportive family and friends to stay on top of things. We have an understanding that if I start acting different or not getting enough sleep, they will ask me about it. I also see a medication manager every six months. I do try to assess myself honestly although I do enjoy a hypomanic state of energy occasionally! I realize the importance of a good night's sleep as being an essential part of my treatment. As my psychiatrist once said, it is my most important medicine. This is hard for me because I enjoy staying up late! I have found I do best on six to seven hours of sleep at night. Any more than that makes me feel sluggish throughout the day.

Miles has been such a blessing to our family. He has always been a cheerful and happy boy. We call him Smiley Miles.

He has had some challenges though, as we knew there would be a possibility since many of these types of illnesses are influenced by genetics. He had large motor skill and speech delays. He didn't walk until he was seventeen and a half months old and really only began talking at age three and a half. He was in the Birth to 3 Program that helped work with him weekly on developing his walking and talking. He has trouble socially, not understanding the "bubble of space" each person has. This has caused problems with other kids and their parents who perceive him as trying to hurt their child. He doesn't have a mean bone is his body! Coming up close and sometimes slapping someone seemed to be his way of saying hi or let's play, especially when he wasn't talking yet.

Communications and friendships were hard because of his speech delay. He had some very obsessive-compulsive behaviors. He liked repetitive playing with the same object for hours at a time. His first main obsession, which lasted several years, was for balloons. He would blow them up and let the air out over and over. He would blow up a huge amount and twist tie them. Then he wanted us to tie them and then untie them again with a fork. There was a shorter fixation on pumping up balls and inflatable toys with the bike pump, deflating and then pumping them up again. Sharpening pencils and crayons over and over was another, then the obsession with checking the power level of the batteries in various things over and over, even lining them up from highest to least amount of power.

Asking everyone what percentage of power was on their phones or iPads was a short phase. Then of course, certain TV shows he would want to watch only that show over and over. And the latest, Minecraft and Clash of Clans.

Obsessions with strange things, delayed speech, and social unawareness are all characteristics of an autism spectrum disorder. We have had him observed and were told he was somewhere on the spectrum; however, we have no official diagnosis as of yet, (aside from ADHD, which I'm not convinced of). He is currently in second grade, and when he gets to third, they have told us they will need a diagnosis for the school district to continue providing services. He was able to go to a developmental preschool for a year, and the following, he went to the Head Start program. He currently has an IEP in the areas of communications and social, which is due to the communication problems. He is in a program like Levi was, which works on social skills and has lunch and specials with the general education kids.

I will say it again, early intervention is the key to success. My brother has a daughter, who also has autism. He has done a fantastic job getting her into therapy right away once she had a diagnosis. Had he not done that, I'm sure that she would not be doing as well as she is today. It doesn't hurt that she has a wonderful father who would go to the moon and back for her either!

I know that God handpicks parents for these children. I feel honored that God has entrusted Jeremy and me with these special boys to train up to be godly men. Challenging? Yes. Boring? Never. Rewarding? Absolutely! My encouragement for you if you have a child or children with any kind of disability is to love them and make sure they know you love them. These are some of the sweetest, most tenderhearted, and compassionate kids I know. Encourage their strengths to see them excel. Of course, God can (and will!) use their weaknesses for His glory too! Remind them that God can use anyone who has a willing heart to bring glory to His name. So keep pressing on and spend a lot of time in prayer.

Once again, we are faced with the "label," but as with Levi, we know the label won't define Miles either. We trust God can do it again in His life as He has done in mine and Levi's.

10

All Things Work Together for Good

Why do we go through these trials? Why did I get a mental illness and then have children with mental illnesses? Why can't I just be "normal?" Why can't my kids just be typical? I have asked these questions, and I'm sure you have too, of yourself or of a loved one. A very good sermon series I was watching from Andy Stanley called *In the Meantime* addressed this question. It was an excellent set of lessons! I found myself in tears over the story a man told of his struggles with learning his kids had autism. I was feeling the fellowship of suffering. The scripture studied that really hit me was:

"Praise be to the God and Father of our Lord Jesus Christ, the Father of compassion and the God of all comfort, who comforts us in all our troubles, so that we can comfort those in any trouble with the comfort we ourselves receive from God. For just as we share abundantly in the sufferings of Christ, so also our comfort abounds through Christ. If we are distressed, it is for your comfort and salvation; if we are comforted, it is for your comfort, which produces in you patient endurance of the same sufferings we suffer.

And our hope for you is firm, because we know that just as you share in our sufferings, so also you share in our comfort."

—2 Corinthians 1:3–7, NIV

One reason that a good God allows us to go through pain and suffering is so that we can comfort others! Just think about it. When someone sends you a card or asks you how you are doing, even a good friend, family member, or even your own preacher, how does that make you feel? Cared about, yes, but a real connection? Then a person walks in and begins sharing with you about their struggles, and you find out they have been through the same struggle and have gotten through it. Isn't there suddenly a special bond between you and that person?

Those of us suffering from a mental illness are uniquely equipped to comfort those struggling with mental illnesses. Those of us who have children afflicted by some type of disorder are more qualified than anyone to comfort those whose children are affected also. I feel like this in itself is comforting.

Look around at your friends, in your church, or maybe within your own family. Find someone who has been through it and came out on the other side. There is hope. You can get through this. There is a reason to go on. There is a reason to keep your faith in God.

The working together for our good, I now see, is helping us get through things so we can help others. What is the second greatest commandment? Love your neighbor as yourself, right? What better way to love on a person than to share in their sufferings?

> "Do not let any unwholesome talk come out of your mouths, but only what is helpful for building others up according to their needs, that it may benefit those who listen."
>
> —Ephesians 4:29, NIV

As we are suffering, be it ourselves or through comforting others, we are also sharing in the sufferings of Christ. He suffered so He can comfort us for all eternity. He can identify with us in our weaknesses.

> "For we do not have a high priest who is unable to empathize with our weaknesses, but we have one who has been tempted in every way, just as we are—yet he did not sin.
>
> Let us then approach God's throne of grace with confidence, so that we may receive mercy and find grace to help us in our time of need."
>
> —Hebrews 4:15–16, NIV

He has given us the fellowship of suffering. And now we are to share the comfort that we have been given in Him to others.

If you are interested in listening to these messages from Andy Stanley, you can find them at meantimeseries. org. It is a great resource for anyone who is going through a time when you feel like you're stuck and there is nothing you can do to get out of it.

A song I wrote after listening to this series of lessons is below. My prayer is that you can relate to the words, and that it gives you hope.

In the Meantime

Lord, don't let this be reality
My heart pleads take this away from me
It looks like there is no way out
It will be this way forever

I could scream and yell into the sky
Asking you why oh why
I believe You can so why don't you
Let me live the dream I wanted to?

But I've decided
That in the meantime
I will accept this gift from You
Even though I don't want to

I resist because I'm human
And the strength is not in me
So in the meantime
Let Your grace be all I need

Up and down I cycle
I just can't understand
My life was planned out perfect
I was following the plan

But just like that it hit me
My heart was torn in two
No hope it seemed, no reason
Even living for You

But I've decided
That in the meantime
I will accept this gift from you
Even though I don't want to

I resist because I'm human
And the strength is not in me
So in the meantime
Let Your grace be all I need

And now I'm living in the moment
I never could have dreamed
Closer to You than I ever hoped to be

I see a purpose in the pain
To show off Your power and Your strength
A promise that I know still includes me

All because I decided
That in the meantime
I would accept this gift from You
Even though I didn't want to

I resisted because I'm human
And the strength was not in me
I found that in the meantime
Your grace was sufficient for me

I still resist because I'm human
But I won't depend on me
For through all my meantime moments
Your grace still sustains me

Through all my meantime moments
Your grace still sustains me.

Speaking of God using our weaknesses for his glory, I want to talk about some of the good that God has brought about through my illness. My prayer is that you will see that God is still there with you all the way through any trials you may have. I have found by trusting that God is working all things for good for them who love the Lord, He has produced the fruit of perseverance and maturity. God has equipped me with a way to minister to others. The label of a mental illness doesn't define me! God does! And you are no exception!

Weighty Matters

After Levi was born, I gained quite a bit of weight. It wasn't from the pregnancy, but I believe it was due to some of the medications I was taking. They either caused me to not feel full or increased my appetite. I was especially addicted to sugar. I remember making a whole batch of chocolate peanut butter bars and eating them all by myself within a few days and then repeating the process. One of the times, I would eat was late at night, so that only compounded the problem. I was pushing two hundred pounds on my five-foot eight-inch frame.

For a long time, the weight gain didn't even bother me. I don't remember even really caring that much. Until one day, my sweet husband, who had never brought it up before, told me he was concerned for my health. Also that he would help me and support me in changing my habits. I began to see pictures of myself and felt disgusted. I wanted to be in pictures with my son as he was growing up. I didn't want to be embarrassed by how I looked in them. I also loved to scrapbook. So I made the decision that I would lose this weight, starting with finding out the medicine culprit and then eating better.

I was able to go off one of the medications that was sabotaging me. Then I went on a strict diet where I would not eat bread or sugar. I was allowed to have some rice or rice cakes. I switched to diet pop also. Not the healthiest way to lose weight, but it worked for me, and I lost fifty pounds in about three months. My metabolism has always been pretty high, so I'm sure that had something to do with it. I had not exercised during the dieting; however, so I lost a lot of muscle mass. I felt so much better after losing all that weight. It was nice to start caring about myself again. Levi was about three when I got my weight back down. So, yes, I have a lot of scrapbooks with pictures of me in them too.

Shortly after I lost my weight, a friend from church who was working at an exercise place for women approached me. She mentioned that they were hiring and wanted to know if I would be interested. The owner came over to my house, interviewed me, and decided to hire and train me to be an "exercise coach." I would be instructing members on how to use the machines and help motivate them to get healthy. I had not exercised regularly for a very long time, so it was wonderful to have a job where I could exercise and get paid doing it!

It was also fun meeting new people, teaching them to use the machines and visiting with them. I was able to encourage them with the story of my weight loss, which inspired them that they could do it too.

It was a very rewarding job, and I stuck with it. I worked at Curves for about six years. I even met two of my very best friends when I was working there. God blessed me with a fun job where I could do well and build relationships with people. It really helped me come back out of the shell I had been hiding in for the past several years. I was feeling better! My moods remained balanced, and I felt pretty "normal" once again. During my employment at Curves, I also studied and became a certified personal trainer.

My weight maintained for quite some time, as long as I was careful with what I ate. If I felt like I was gaining some weight, I would struggle to gain control of the one thing I knew I could—what I put in my mouth.

I would get in these kicks of forbidding myself any sugar at all, only to find myself a few weeks later bingeing on cookies. I would be fine if I would not succumb to my baker's brain and bake sweets! Then I would feel horrible, give up for a while, get sick of myself, and begin the cycle again. Weight gain and loss has always been a struggle for me.

I am an all or nothing, black or white type of personality. In my experience, it seems like this is true of many people with bipolar. It's either one extreme or the other. I have a very hard time finding balance in my eating, or even in other areas of my life. My biggest struggle has been in moderation. In pretty much all things. I tend to either obsess about it, or I could care less.

So how do I take this annoying part of being bipolar and use it for God's glory? I feel just fine about obsessing over God. To love people and care for their needs. I think we must channel what feels like a weakness and turn it around to bring God glory. Even Paul asked God to take away the thorn he had been given, but God didn't remove it. Paul learned that it was through his weakness that God's power was most mightily displayed. We have been given a gift, something that God is using for a greater good than we ourselves can even see. Get to know God deeply. Use that fire you have within to kindle your relationship with Him.

I can testify that God has used me to effectively reach out and help others who are having the same kinds of struggles I do. I find that people are more likely to open up with someone who has been through a similar life situation. Like I've mentioned, there is definitely a level of comfort and safety in being able to confide in someone who has been there, has genuine empathy, and understands the struggles. I have heard about many people who have struggled with different difficulties in their lives and then pursued a career in counseling or psychiatry. These professionals make it much easier for a client to relax and speak openly. I find that for me, it is so much more real to share my story so that people who think I don't have any problems can understand that "you can't judge a book by its cover," as the old cliché goes.

I have had the opportunity to teach Bible studies a few times a month at the women's and children's shelter at our local Union Gospel Mission. I try to be honest and willing to share my experiences if the subject comes up. I have befriended many of the women, and some of them have become dear friends of mine. Had I not been through the trials of depression and mania, I know I would not be effective at reaching others in these situations to show them the love Jesus has for them. Because of my story, women have opened up and shared their stories with me. It's really all about building relationships. When people feel loved and accepted right where they are, it leaves an impression. "By this everyone will know that you are my disciples, if you love one another" (John 13:35, NIV). The trials of my life have worked together for good and brought glory to God, and so can yours. In the meantime, know that God is not absent. God is not angry. Things will get better. Trust God that He will help you push through the heavy gloom because on the other side waits a stronger, more mature Christian who can use that struggle for God's glory.

Growing Spiritually

Now I would like to share with you some of the things I have learned over the years on my spiritual walk that have been helpful to me. As I said previously, with mental illness comes obsessive thinking. Focusing on loving God and loving people has directed my life toward laying up treasures in heaven for eternity. If you have to be obsessed with something, make it Jesus!

One of my favorite—and most sobering—illustrations I have ever seen is from Francis Chan, the author of the book *Crazy Love*. In his "rope illustration," he brings out a long rope on stage. The rope has a six-inch red piece colored at the end. He states that this red piece of the rope represents our time on earth. People put so much energy and emphasis on this little block of time we have on earth, accumulating things and saving up money so they can retire and live comfortably for that last little few inches of the red part. But we forget about what comes after the red part. He then says that the rest of the rope represents eternity. If we believe that our souls live on forever and ever in one of two places, then why are we so concerned about this little piece in time? Our life on earth is but a vapor. We don't spend much time contemplating eternity, which never ends.

It's a hard thing to take in, but the overwhelming fact is, it's a reality. As Christians, we believe a soul will spend eternity in either heaven or hell. Christ tells us to lay up our treasures in heaven, which is eternal, instead of on earth, which is temporary. He doesn't promise this will be easy, but He does promise it will be worth it!

So I have chosen to focus on developing spiritual maturity and on making disciples of Jesus. In Matthew, Jesus tells us our purpose as Christians:

> "Then Jesus came to them and said, "All authority in heaven and on earth has been given to me. Therefore go and make disciples of all nations, baptizing them in the name of the Father and of the Son and of the Holy Spirit, and teaching them to obey everything I have commanded you. And surely I am with you always, to the very end of the age."
>
> —Matthew 28:18-20, NIV

These are His last words spoken before He ascended into heaven. I think we really tend to listen to a person's last words as they pass away from this earth. So how much more attentive should we be to Jesus's words, one who died and rose again?

I have tried to live out that great commission in my life. Not because I feel a duty or obligation, but because I am thankful to God and what He has done for me in Christ Jesus. If we really believe what we say we believe—that Jesus is the answer for the world—are we living like we believe that?

Do we care enough about lost people that we are willing to step out of our comfort zone? This is a question I asked myself. I made the decision and fervently prayed for the Holy Spirit to lead me to whatever He wanted me to do, to be whatever He wanted me to be, no matter the cost. I've heard it said that this "is a scary prayer to pray because the Spirit might lead me where I don't really want to go." So how willing are you?

I want to share with you just how far the Spirit has led me, to show you that God will use you if you are willing, no matter if you have a mental illness! You've read my story. I've been there. And I could quite possibly be there again someday. Lord willing, I won't, but that's where trusting God comes in. Hanging on to His promises. I am living proof that there is hope, and that hope can only be found in Christ. Cling to Him and never let go.

> "Resist the devil and he will flee from you. Come near to God and He will come near to you."
>
> —James 4:7b-8a, NIV

> "Do not be anxious about anything, but by prayer and petition with thanksgiving, present your requests to God, and the peace of God, which transcends all understanding, will guide your hearts and your minds in Christ Jesus."
>
> —Philippians 4:6–7, NIV

The Lord has taken me on an amazing journey! Before Miles was born, I did some ministry for several years running the free clothing bank, Christ's Closet, at our church. I didn't want to see such a great community ministry closed, so I volunteered to be in charge. Also, I got involved in being a study helper for World Bible School, a free Bible study program available by web study or mail. This enabled me to study with people who had already expressed interest in learning and were willing to study diligently.

For quite some time, I had felt God tugging at my heart to teach a Bible study at the women's shelter. I had served lunch there once a week for a lengthy period of time, while Miles was in preschool a few days a week, but I wanted to be more involved. When I first inquired, the times they had available would not work out with the schedule I had with my family and school schedule. Once Miles began Head Start, I wasn't even able to volunteer serving lunch. So I took the step to e-mail the volunteer coordinator that I was interested in teaching a Bible study. The chaplain called me and asked me to come have a tour and talk about what the position entailed. I went in and agreed to teaching on Saturdays, two to three times a month. I am still teaching the wonderful ladies there twice a month. God has used this local ministry in amazing ways.

I feel especially called to minister to people in these situations; many of whom suffer from mental illnesses. I feel like I can relate in many ways to them, as a sort of fellowship in suffering. I have shared my story with the women there, and they have been very open and seem to enjoy having me there to teach. A few ladies from my church family are also enjoying coming and participating in the Bible study and visiting with the women. For a while, I was driving the church van over to pick people up to come to our worship services and would love to start that up again involving more people.

Several women have come to our church and become Christians. We were able to rent our guest room to a woman and her daughter for three months to help them get back on their feet. They both became Christians. I feel that this is a huge way God has used the situations I have gone through for His good, to expand His kingdom and bring Him glory.

The other way God has used me ended up involving Jeremy and Levi. One day, I got a Facebook friend request from the preacher of the H.B. Colony Church of Christ in Vijayawada, India. We started chatting on Facebook. He was looking for some sponsors for children at an orphanage he had started and was overseeing. He gave me some names and phone numbers of people here in the States who come to India on a yearly basis, so I could check out his credibility. After checking out their references, we began supporting some orphan children there at Elnora Orphan Home. Soon, Raja, his wife, Kumari, and their family began to Skype with us regularly.

After a little while, Raja asked if I would be willing to teach their ladies Bible class if he translated for me. I accepted the offer, and I am so glad I did! I started doing that on a weekly basis. Their study was on Friday evenings, so because they are thirteen and a half hours ahead of us there, I would get up early Friday mornings and teach. I had always wanted to do foreign missions, and here I was, teaching a Bible class in India! Technology sure has come a long ways!

Raja asked if I would be willing to teach the Gospel to some Hindu people who were interested in learning about Jesus. I felt so unprepared! I bumbled my way through the lesson I had put together, and the Holy Spirit must have been at work, because at the end, someone expressed that they would like to study more about Christianity and baptism! A few days later, he asked me to teach some people again, and a few more expressed real interest!

I was amazed at how God was using me to teach people about Jesus. It's contagious. I just want to experience the feeling of bringing people to Christ more and more! It is exciting to me when I think about the "butterfly effect" of one person's actions reaching to affect so many people. Knowing I have been a part of Christ's mission for us makes me feel fulfilled.

After about a year of teaching and visiting with Raja's family on Skype, Raja mentioned that they were working on raising the funds to build a new home for the orphans. They were renting two buildings at the time, housing fifty-four children. The new building was to support at least 150 orphans. He also wants to have a Christian school there at the building and said he wanted to honor me by naming it after me. They had named the orphan home after the wife of one of the preachers who came there yearly. This is a way they show their appreciation for people that they want to honor.

Then Raja asked if we would come there to visit sometime. We laughed about that for a little while, because we really didn't see how that would be possible for us to do. It would be great, but I wasn't sure if Jeremy would really want to go. So we said maybe someday and left it at that.

But, as God would have it, in February of 2013, we bought Jeremy, Levi, and me each a ticket for India! We would be going there at the end of December through the beginning of January and staying for a little over two weeks. We were hoping the orphan home would be completed by then, but construction was stopped part way through for lack of funds.

We got passports, visas, immunizations, and all the necessities for overseas travel. We also made arrangements for Miles to stay with Jeremy's parents while we were in India. I couldn't believe this was going to happen! It didn't seem like a reality until we actually got on the plane and were on our way.

The main thing that really scared me was the time change and how we should take our medications. I did not want our bodies to get out of balance. But God was faithful! He helped Levi and me to do very well for the most part. I did have a small panic attack when we were there, but I think my body was still adjusting to the thirteen-and-a-half-hour time change. Our days and nights were flip-flopped. The other thing was that I would get nauseous quite often whenever we were traveling by car. The traffic there is unlike any I have ever seen! Peppermint candies were my best friend whenever we drove around anywhere.

We were honored with handmade flower garland leis when we arrived at the airport and whenever we entered a church gospel meeting. They treated us like a king, queen, and prince. At the conclusion of the women's conference, they placed leis around our necks, shawls on our shoulders, and crowns on our heads. This felt like we were being honored far beyond what they should do, but this is their culture and their way of showing appreciation. The Hindu people were very tolerant of Christianity in the area where we were, and the Muslim population was very low. We didn't feel like we were in danger while we were there.

It was very heartbreaking to see what their lives were like there in the villages. My heart went out to the people as I compared my circumstances in life to theirs and thought about the many things I take for granted. Even something as simple as a toilet was unheard of in the villages. We felt spoiled going back to our hotel when we had seen how little these people had. But despite everything, they were joyful. It was very humbling.

Jeremy and I had the opportunity to speak to hundreds of people in India about the Gospel of Jesus Christ. It was absolutely amazing! Many were Hindus or from other religious groups. We went from village to village holding gospel meetings. They organized a ladies conference for two days while we were there, with me as the featured guest speaker. They had even made a huge poster with my picture on it to advertise. The first day, about five hundred were in attendance, and the second day, there were around six hundred! We worked with translators as we taught, which was very nice, since you could pause every so often to gather your thoughts in between translations.

The people were so receptive to the Gospel! We heard that thirty-eight people gave their lives to Christ and were baptized, and more were still studying as a result of our coming and teaching God's Word! Even if only one person decided to become a Christian, the whole trip would have been worth it.

Near the end of our stay, we met up with three men from the U.S. who were just beginning their annual visit. It was nice to be able to get to know them and learn about the ministries they were involved in there and other places. They work very hard training the men in the Bible to prepare them for teaching others about the Good News. I also found out that I was the first woman from a mission team to come there to India, since none of their wives had ever been before. God used me to pave the way, because several women are planning to go this year. It is amazing to think of all the lives that will be affected this year because they will be holding a three-day women's conference while the mission team is there. Knowing I was a part of making that happen blows me away! I sometimes wonder if, at the end of our earthly lives, God will allow us to see how many lives each of us have personally touched for His glory.

Would I have ever dreamt I would go to India? I wouldn't have believed you if you had told me a few years ago that I would be called to go to India. But the truth was, when I opened my heart and asked the Spirit to lead me, wherever He could use me and in whatever way, I never could have imagined doing what we did!

Levi was able to have the opportunity to share the Gospel with the orphan children. Raja's son, Timothy, translated. What a life-changing experience for my fourteen-year-old! He did a great job, despite his shyness in front of crowds. We all got to meet and play with the children at the home, as well as tour the unfinished building.

Of course, I had to go shopping. The ladies took me out for some traditional Indian clothing, and Kumari bought me several outfits, including a lovely sari. I also picked out a sari for myself. We went to a night market where they sold all sorts of handmade things and also had a wax museum about Indian culture.

We all grew so much spiritually from that trip to India. It was so exhilarating going from village to village all day, knowing we were doing the will of God. There was nothing we would have rather done. When we returned home, it was a letdown as we were so used to sharing the Gospel with people who are willing to listen, seeing the fruit of our labor right before our eyes. With all of the Hindu and Muslim influence, the people who became Christians would most likely be cut off from their families. So if you become a Christian there, it's all or nothing. You don't see that in America. Sadly enough, saying you're a Christian here often doesn't mean the same as it does there.

12

What Can I Do?

Ministry can be messy. And sometimes we don't want to get involved. But remember, these are people. These are souls. And they need to know Jesus.

Just being willing to take a look around and actually "see" people is a huge first step. Evangelism is highly relational. It can be as simple as getting to know someone, really know them. Begin to share your life with them, and don't leave the God parts out. You never know where the conversations will go. God will always work in your efforts to share Jesus because the Spirit was sent to help us be a witness to others. Just pray for the right words. You don't have to stand on a street corner and shout at people. It's all about building relationships. People are more likely to listen to a friend who is genuinely concerned about them than a stranger who preaches hellfire and brimstone! We don't want to scare people into believing, but to show them the hope we have in Christ!

We will never feel like we are "ready" to study with people. Just like you're never "ready" to have children, then the baby comes and your world changes. Having children is usually not exactly what we had imagined. It's a lot of work! But that child is worth it all. If you know how to be a friend and share your life story and relationship with God, you can make disciples. But relationships take work, so be willing to invest time and possibly even money. Sometimes God will ask you to step out of your comfort zone. Trust God to help you. I definitely didn't feel qualified to teach! But I tried, and God blessed my meager efforts.

What are some practical ways you can get involved in your church and spread the news of Jesus? I will list several ideas below that have helped me. I hope they will be an encouragement to you and help you to see you are a useful part of the body of Christ!

- You may be called to minister to other people with a mental illness or create awareness in your church or city. Our church recently began a mental health awareness group to help people understand different types of illnesses and learn ways to be a support to those affected by them.
- Build friendships with nonbelievers.
- Share your story. It doesn't matter where you are in your journey. When you share, "don't leave the God parts out," as a good preacher friend of mine says. Just share what God is doing in you.

- Love and serve people when you notice you are focusing on yourself too much. Shift your attention outward. Show compassion unconditionally to all people, not showing favoritism.
- Get other people to join in. If they see you trying even though you don't feel "qualified," they will be more willing. Grow together!
- Remember that when you were baptized into Christ, you became a member of the body of Christ, the church. "For we were all baptized by one Spirit so as to form one body" (1 Corinthians 12:13a, NIV). Remember, the body needs you as much as you need them! We were made to have community with other believers.
- Use your struggles to help others who are struggling with the same things. There is a special connection between fellow sufferers. This all comes back to getting to know people. We can't help people when we don't know anything about them.
- Don't just talk about it! Jump in and do something when you see an opportunity to help out.
- Start being a study helper for an online Bible study such as World Bible School. As I mentioned before, these people already want to study, so there's half the work done already for you! As you study, you will learn more and provide them direction by sending them Bible lessons and correcting and answering their questions from their studies. This is also a great way to build relationships, especially if you are an introverted

person and have a hard time thinking quickly to answer people. With WBS, you can think about your answers before you reply to a student or even ask others their opinions if you aren't sure. Go to worldbibleschool.org to learn how to be a study helper! Or even take the classes yourself to grow spiritually.

- Do a free online spiritual gifts survey, like on SpiritualGiftsTest.com, to find out the things you are good at and plug into those areas in your church family. Don't look at others and wish you had their gifts. Focus on learning what you can do as a part of the body.

Straight Talk

I definitely don't have it all together! But I trust in the one who does. To help you, I want to tell you about the things that have been helpful to keep myself stable for the past several years.

- *My relationship with God.* Prayer journaling has been a wonderful way to talk to God and to keep my mind from wandering. Plus, you can look back and see answers to prayers, which is an amazing faith-builder! You can also write down when God answers a specific prayer in your life so you won't forget it.

- *A good support system.* If you don't have a supportive family, find some people whom you trust, preferably from your church. Attend a support group. Have friends or family you trust help keep you accountable, and be honest when you are having problems.

- *Staying on my medications.* This is such a hard one, especially with bipolar disorder. I can't stress enough to stay on your meds! Since I have been stable for a majority of the time after discovering I have bipolar disorder, I can tell you it is because of the above things combined with staying on my medications that I know are helping me. Mental illnesses are tricky. You may feel better, so you might convince yourself that you are healed. But the reason you feel better is because the medications are balancing out the chemicals in your brain! Trust me, I have been there. During my pregnancy with Levi I thought I would be just fine off my meds. Going off your medications just makes things worse. If you don't feel like things are working right, see your doctor to get your "cocktail" tweaked.

- *Consistent med management and counseling therapy.* Even if you are stable, see your medicine manager at least every six months. Commit to giving him or her a call if you are experiencing more symptoms in between appointments.

- *Get enough rest!* (I'm still working on this one).

- *Stay aware of triggers and symptoms.* Ask your husband, wife, family member, or friend who knows you best to let you know if they notice anything different in your behavior. Make the

decision beforehand to listen to them. They are
there to help, not point out all your flaws.

- *I got involved in something outside of myself.*
  Especially during depression.
- *Be in the Word of God daily.* Praying scriptures to
  God and even posting verses around the house
  as reminders.
- *Live in the moment.* Focus on what you are doing
  right now instead of what you did or will do. This
  especially helps with depression, when you feel
  a sort of detachment from reality. One thing I
  learned in the hospital was especially helpful:
  when you start worrying, visualize a stop sign to
  remind yourself to live in the here and now.

Child of God

Identity

Ever longing
Wishing, hoping
Laid back, easygoing
My ambition to be
Uptight, stiff, and serious
My traits all too apparent
Gladly given up
For a taste of happiness
Why can't I be content
With what God has instilled in me?
Realization washes over me
And I know my place
Is the way He made me

We can try to find our identity in all sorts of things. Maybe we find our worth based on our looks, personality, a job, our family, our hobbies, failures, religion, or even our illnesses. But the only thing that matters is that you see yourself the way God sees you. He sees you as His child. If you are a Christian, you are a part of His family, adopted as His own.

The world feeds us the lies that you have to be this way or that way to be loved and accepted. I have fallen into that trap like a majority of others, and it's not fun. Then the comparing starts, and there is no way to win at that game. There will always be someone smarter, prettier, and wealthier. I could go on and on. When all you are hearing is the screaming of the media to "lose weight," "look younger," or "make more money," it's easy to drown out the Spirit. What we have to do is keep "…fixing our eyes on Jesus, the pioneer and perfecter of faith." (Hebrews 12:2a, NIV).

I find this comparison trap especially hard for people with mental illness. We see people who look like their life is perfect, their kids are perfect, and their body is perfect. Our minds go wild and overthink things, building up things to be much more complicated in our minds. When someone looks at us funny or even maybe doesn't say "hi" or act the way we think they should, we take it so personally and then try to analyze everything about the interaction. And where does it get us? Absolutely nowhere!

I am learning to see myself as a child of God, made in the image of God, just the way He wants me to be. I can take care of myself spiritually, mentally, and physically, being a good steward of what God has given me. But it is no use beating myself up about what I am not or trying to figure out how I can be more _____ (fill in the blank). As long as I can honestly say I am doing the best that I can with what God has given me, then I should be happy with that. If I am not, then I need to take an honest look at myself and get my mind back in sync with God's Word.

But sometimes, things just seem like way more than we can handle. What about the saying that "God won't give you more than you can handle"? I used to be comforted by that statement, until I recently learned that God does *not* promise that. Let's look at that scripture.

> "No temptation has overtaken you except what is common to mankind. And God is faithful; he will not let you be tempted beyond what you can bear. But when you are tempted, he will also provide a way out so that you can endure it."
>
> —1 Corinthians 10:13, NIV

God *does* give us more than we can handle. That is, more than we can handle *on our own*. He wants us to turn to Him when things are terrible, when we feel awful about ourselves, helpless or hopeless. If I thought God won't give me more than I can handle, why would I need God? He brings us to these times to draw us back to Him, cause us to depend solely on Him. And we will become more mature Christians when we are through.

So my encouragement for you is to use your illness for the glory of God. Do not let the label of a mental disorder stop you from serving God! You are a child of God. That is your name! Take the comfort God has given you in Christ Jesus and persevere. Find someone who has made it through similar circumstances and gain comfort through that. Then step outside of yourself and comfort someone else who is going through the same thing.

I have been there, and there is a light at the end of the tunnel. Don't give up. God can and will use you in amazing ways if you will allow Him to. Thank you for letting me share my story with you.

The Tunnel

One day I'll be through this
One day all will see
Because I've made it through this trial
I am now a better me.

It's hard to see the light
Shining so far ahead
The tunnel is so dim and bleak
I'm thinking, *Am I dead?*

But I know that God will take me
Through the storm where I am cast
And one day he'll appear again
To take me home at last!

And so, until that day arrives
Forever I will stand
By His side eternally
Holding His unchanging hand.

(November 20, 1999)

15

The Gospel in a Nutshell

I want to share with you the gospel presentation that I prepared and gave to the people of India. This is the message I used that was translated line by line into their language, Telugu:

Hello! My name is Kayla. I am visiting from the United States. Today, I want to share with you the most important thing to me. It is the good news of what the God of the Bible has done for us through His Son, Jesus Christ. If you are not familiar with this God, I hope you will listen with an open mind and heart today.

Let's start at the beginning. In Genesis, the first book in the Old Testament, it records the beginning of the world. When God created the world, He created a perfect paradise! Everything was good. There was only peace and goodness and love. Imagine a world without physical pain—no sadness, no death.

This was what the Garden of Eden was, a paradise! Adam and his wife, Eve, were the first man and woman God created. They lived in the garden with all the animals and beautiful creations God had made, were naked, and felt no shame, and believe it or not, God even walked and talked with Adam and Eve!

They had everything they needed to be happy. God and man coexisted in peace with one another. God gave them only one rule they had to follow: They were told not to eat from one tree in the garden, the tree of the knowledge of good and evil.

Adam and Eve didn't even have any idea what evil was. One day though, the devil, in the form of a snake, came to Eve and told her that she would become wise like God if she ate some of the fruit from the tree they were supposed to stay away from.

She did and gave some to Adam, and he ate it too. Once they ate this fruit, their eyes were opened, and they realized they were naked and felt ashamed. In fact, they hid from God and made coverings for themselves. It was like a switch came on in their brains, and they all of a sudden knew right from wrong. They, for the first time, felt guilt and shame.

This is when sin entered the world. Sin is anything that we do that does not measure up to the perfect standard of God. When sin came in, the relationship between God and man was broken. They had not trusted that God knew best. Instead they thought maybe God was hiding something good from them. But God was protecting them from sin.

We sin when we decide *we* know what's better for us than God does, so instead of listening to Him, we do what *we* want to. It's like we are telling God we don't trust Him. A relationship cannot exist without trust. So Adam and Eve had to leave the garden, never to return.

So now we have the problem of sin in the world, bringing death, pain, fear, and hate. Things that God did not want for us! He knew this would happen, and He had a plan even from the beginning. He made a way to repair the relationship between God and man (Ephesians 1:3–14). Because of Adam, we are all born into sin. We all inherit it (Romans 5:12). And because of this, we are all sinners (Romans 3:23).

In the Old Testament, God established laws for His chosen people, the Jews, which included sacrificing animals for their sins. But this way of "being forgiven" did not really get rid of our sin completely. There had to be a perfect sacrifice once for all. The laws and the prophets of the Old Testament were only pointing to God's perfect plan.

At just the right time, God sent His Son Jesus to come down, to be born of a virgin woman, to live a sinless life (Galatians 4:1–7). There were many prophecies about a Messiah who was to come, and Jesus fulfilled all of them, but the Jews rejected Jesus as the Messiah. They did not recognize Him as the Savior.

They were expecting an earthly king, who would set up an earthly kingdom, a kingdom where the Israelites would be in control of things. But Christ came to establish a heavenly kingdom, which was hard for them to believe or even understand. The leaders especially felt threatened. So they had Him crucified on a cross. A cross was a horrible and painful death.

It was God's will for this to happen. Because the only way to undo what Adam did was to have Jesus die on a cross, that is what He did. He took all of our sin upon Himself because He loves us. He did this while we were still sinful (Romans 5:8). Even before we were sorry for anything! A perfect sacrifice had to be made to undo the sin Adam committed (Romans 5:19). This is true mercy and grace.

As we know, when Adam sinned, the relationship between God and man was broken. When Jesus came, He came to repair this, to bring us back in the right relationship with God again. He did this by dying on a cross, in which God allowed for all sin of mankind be put upon Jesus. He was buried, and after the third day, He rose again, with no sin!

So this illustration shows how God accomplished His plan:

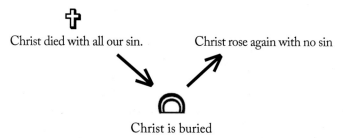

Christ died with all our sin.　　Christ rose again with no sin

Christ is buried

Romans 6:10 says that He died for our sins, once for all—all our past, present, and future sins. And so now, with our sins forgiven, we can be in a right relationship with God again. Only Jesus makes this possible. God wins us back to Him because of His great love and sacrifice for us.

Now we can either accept this as truth or reject it. I hope that you will accept it though!

One way you can respond is in rejecting Jesus and insisting on being in control of yourself. Imagine a throne. When I am in control of my life, it is like I am the one sitting on the throne. When I am on the throne, I make my own decisions, I set my own priorities, I choose how I want to talk, I choose how to spend my money, I choose how I act in my relationships. It's all about me. I won't ask anyone else what I should do because I want to be in charge of my own life. But when we are living for ourselves, it doesn't always work out so well, does it?

We can also respond in a somewhat "religious" way, hoping the good we have done in our lives outweighs the bad. We try to "earn" our way to heaven. The truth is, in God's eyes, there are never enough good things you could do that can erase even one bad thing we do!

Let's read Romans 3:10, NIV. "There is no one righteous, not even one;" Romans 6:23 tells us that sin leads to death. Any time there is sin, it has to be atoned for. When you break one part of the law, you've broken all the laws (James 2:10). This is why we can't ever earn our way back to God on good behavior. Once again, this is another me-centered belief, based on what I can do.

People usually are not willing to change until they realize that these ways don't work. So what happens when we are tired of this way of living for ourselves and depending on ourselves to be "good enough" to hopefully save us? We must finally surrender to God.

To surrender means to give up. We admit we can't rule our lives or be good enough to fix this and get right with God again. We make the decision to believe that Jesus Christ is God's Son and accept what He did for us on the cross to pay for our sins. We give our lives back to Him.

So how does God's Word teach us that we can get back in a right relationship with God again? How can we be forgiven of our sins? (Romans 5:1) How can we become justified before God? How can we be sinless before God?

First, we must believe and accept what Jesus did for us (Romans 10:9–10). We must repent of our sins, which means to recognize we have sinned and decide we don't want to do this anymore (Acts 17:30).

But does it stop there? Some say you just must say a prayer and ask Christ Jesus into your heart, but this is not found anywhere in Scripture. We have to look at the scriptures all together, not just partly. We have already looked at the verses that speak about salvation in Romans 10, but let's go back a few chapters and see what Paul, the writer of Romans, had to say about it.

Let's read Romans 6:3–4, NIV

"Or don't you know that all of us who were baptized into Christ Jesus were baptized into His death? We were therefore buried through baptism into death in order that, just as Christ was raised from the dead through the glory of the Father, we too may live a new life."

Here we are talking about what happens when we are baptized or "immersed," which means to be dipped under and come back up in water. It is our way of mirroring in our own lives what God did for us.

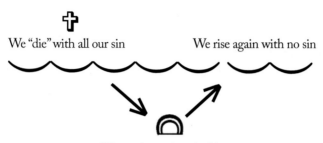

We "die" with all our sin   We rise again with no sin

We are buried with Christ

So when we are baptized, we are "copying" in a sense what Jesus did, and we are obeying what He commands us to do, right before He ascended back into heaven (Mark 16:16; Matthew 28:18–20). We would do well to obey what He told us to do. Jesus says "If you love me, keep my commands" (John 14:15, NIV).

The forgiveness and grace is a free gift from God, and it is the work He does that saves us (Colossians 2:11–12). There is nothing we can do to earn it. It is like if someone handed you a trillion- dollar check, you never could earn that much in a lifetime! But what do you have to do to receive that check? You have to take it to the bank and deposit it into your account. This is what happens when we are baptized. We are not "earning our salvation by works," but it is at baptism that we are accepting His gift of salvation. Let's read some examples of some people who were moved to faith in Jesus in the New Testament:

- The first sermon preached by Peter in Acts 2:36–42.
- The Ethiopian Eunuch and Philip in Acts 8:26–39.

In these stories, did they know a lot about Jesus or being a Christ follower before they were baptized? No, they didn't! You don't have to know a lot either, only that you believe that Jesus is the son of God that you want to follow Him for the rest of your life by surrendering your life over to Him. This means to be sorry for the things you have done that are not pleasing to God and deciding to not do those things anymore.

This is the start of your relationship with God. Baptism is like a wedding ceremony between you and God. For example, when you hear about Jesus and are learning what God has done for you, it is like you are "dating" God. Then it comes to a point where you accept Him and decide you want to follow Him, similar to being engaged. Some people simply say a prayer, asking Jesus into their hearts. But as I mentioned before, this way of salvation is not found anywhere in the Bible. If we are simply engaged to be married, are you considered "married" yet? No, not until that day that you stand before Him and confess your belief in Him, and as you are baptized, it is like a vow of commitment to Jesus. Just as the marriage ceremony marks the real beginning of the most intimate relationship we can have on earth, your baptism marks the real beginning of the most intimate relationship you will ever have—a relationship with God.

God had to sacrifice His own perfect son so that He can recognize us as His own when we are "clothed in Christ" at baptism (Galatians 3:26–28). It is at baptism we are forgiven of our sin as we read in Acts 2:38 earlier.

God now adopts us into His family because He no longer sees our imperfections but only Jesus's perfection. We are now children of God and cannot only call Him our Father, but even more intimate than that, our *dad*. That is the kind of relationship He wants with us.

Now when God looks at you, it is as if Jesus is standing between you and God, and all He can see is Jesus's perfection, because our sins are covered by Jesus's blood. He is now our mediator between us and God (1 Timothy 2:5). We do not need to have anyone else come to God on our behalf, only Jesus Christ.

When we talk to God in prayer, read His Word, and show our faith by our actions, we are doing our part in the relationship too. A one-sided relationship is not a relationship. Both people have to participate, and that's what makes us closer. Just as when you are married, you keep getting to know your husband or wife. The same is true with God. "Come near to God and He will come near to you" (James 4:7, NIV). So how do we start "coming near" to God?

As we rise up out of the waters of baptism, we are a new creation in Christ! (2 Corinthians 5:17) Now instead of me on the throne, *Jesus* is on the throne. God's Holy Spirit is put into us and guides and helps us to follow Jesus.

Now He guides my decisions, my words, my priorities, my money, and my relationships. It is now a religion of love, not fear. We are now brought back into a right relationship with God again, just like he intended it to be in the beginning. We receive the Holy Spirit at baptism, and He helps guide us.

Are we still going to sin? Yes! But we must keep walking in faith, and Jesus will continue to wash away our sins (1 John 1:5–10).

"Jesus answered, "I am the way and the truth and the life. No one comes to the Father except through Me." (John 14:6, NIV). "Therefore, there is now no condemnation for those who are *in* Christ Jesus," (Romans 8:1, NIV. Emphasis mine.)

When you are baptized into Christ, you become part of the body of believers, the church of Christ (1 Corinthians 12:12–13). You have now been born into the family of God and have the support of your fellow brothers and sisters in Christ locally and throughout the world!

If you are ready to make this commitment to confess your belief in Jesus and would like to be baptized for the forgiveness of your sins and to receive the gift of the Holy Spirit, who will guide you as you live your life as a follower of Jesus and confirm your salvation, or if you would like to learn more or want to ask for prayers, please come forward now.

Who's on the Throne Again?

There have been times when I have come up with an idea that I really think would be pleasing to God. Then I would find out later that it wasn't in God's plan for my life or my family. I got this great idea of how we should become houseparents for a children's home. We even had an interview where all four of us went to visit for several days. We loved the people and the idea of what we would be doing, but for whatever reason, it just wasn't God's timing. I had told God I really wanted to do this and asked Him to show us clearly if it was what we should do. I can see now that I had pushed the idea even when there were some signs early on that should have been red flags. Jeremy and I agreed we would go if they asked us, so we waited for their answer, which we knew was going to be God's answer. They sent us a letter that said they loved our family and thought we would be great houseparents, but not right now. They wanted us to concentrate on our own kids, as they felt if we went there, they would not get the attention they needed from us. Though it was heartbreaking, we knew it was God's answer. Deep down, I knew He was right, that it wasn't the right time. At least it was a "wait" instead of a "no."

But then, I started thinking the fault was because of my bipolar or Levi's issues or even Miles's problems that were surfacing. Why did we even bring our kids? If we had not brought them, would they have asked us to come? We should have gone all alone! It was tempting to remain bitter and angry at myself, the boys, or the children's home because I felt like we were being discriminated against. Looking back, although it was a gut-wrenching disappointment, I see some reasons why God wanted to keep us here in the Tri-Cities. Levi got into the Delta STEM school as I said before, which will equip him for his future. We were able to be there for some of our friends who really needed us in their times of crisis. I can see Jeremy and me being houseparents someday, but God wants us to be here for our kids right now. It also showed us some areas of our marriage that we needed to work on, which was a blessing that came out of the whole experience. Plus, we probably just weren't ready for it yet!

When I reflect on it, I can see a difference between how God placed the opportunities with the mission and India right in my lap, but how I had forced my will to get the opportunity for the houseparent job. It was a good learning experience though, and it taught me some good things. Once again, good coming from an upsetting trial.

So I have determined I will not just come up with my own big ministry ideas anymore. Of course, it's mainly because I hate to get my hopes up only to have them crash down. But instead, I have decided that I will wait upon the Lord and see what He leads me to, instead of jumping ahead and trying to be in control. I also pray for clarity, because I'm normally not a very observant person.

If you or a loved one ever feels discriminated against because of your illness, I know and understand how you feel! It feels unfair! Even these people were Christians, why couldn't they give us a chance? Whatever happened to unconditional love?

We have to remember that God is still in control, no matter how much we may try to manipulate our way into the driver's seat. We are all human, and it is the nature of sin to want to be in charge. I have to keep reminding myself every day though, *Get off the throne, Kayla! You made Jesus Lord, remember?*

I wrote this song back in 1996, before my depression hit. I believe that God gave me this song because He knew I was going to have this power struggle with Him time and time again. Maybe it will strike a chord in your heart like it still does every time I read the words.

Let Him Take Control

Sometimes in this life
Things don't go my way
I make up all sorts of plans
But I forget about today

I get caught up in thinking
About my hopes and dreams
But I'm not the master of my life
God has His own schemes

God says not to worry
About tomorrow
But I can't help from wondering
About the things He has in store
So I have to remind myself
To let Him take control

It appears that when I plan things
Backfiring seems to be
The main course of action
That happens to me

So I must remember
When I'm thinking far ahead
To keep my feet on solid ground
Not forgetting what He said

God says not to worry
About tomorrow
But I can't help from wondering
About the things He has in store
So I have to remind myself
To let Him take control

Worry's not the answer
It doesn't change a thing
Our God, He does not change His mind
Just because we're wondering

Just to let Him take control
That's my only prayer
Giving back the life He gave to me
To put it in His care

God says not to worry
About tomorrow
But I can't help from wondering
About the things He has in store
So I have to remind myself
To let Him take control

(May, 1996)

It's a God Thing

Another thing that has helped me spiritually is seeing the answers to prayer. This builds my faith up so much! Writing in my prayer journal, I can keep an account of what I have prayed for and the answers. This helps remind me in times of doubt that God is faithful.

Answered prayers are amazing. I can just look back and remember that God has always provided for us monetarily whenever we needed it. One time when this happened, it just blew me out of the water. You know, when something is just a God thing? This was it.

Jeremy had just finished nursing school and had gotten a job as an RN at a nursing home. He had been working for the school district as a custodian up until the end of the month, and then he would start the new job. There was something in the timing that we were going to be about $1,000 short on the bills for that month. I remember just having the confidence that God would get us through, so I don't remember really worrying (and that was surprising even to myself!).

The time we needed the money was still a few weeks away, and I remember going to the mailbox one day and receiving a check from Washington State for Levi's disability we had gotten him on. Opening the envelope, there was a check for $980! I remember thinking, *No way, this can't be real! They made a mistake.* They had to have made a mistake. We had normally been getting less than $300 a month for Levi. So I called up the Washington State Disability Office. I was told it was back pay from the months previous that we should have been getting a higher amount! We were floored.

Especially from that time on, if I start to get an inkling of worry about money, I first examine to see if we are using it wisely. If not, we can tweak it here or there. But if we are honestly doing the best we can, and being faithfully generous, I think of this story and wait to see what God will do next. And He has never disappointed us!

Just recently, when we were running a little short before payday, Miles walked over and pulled out a crisp, new $100 bill out of my purse. It was just lying loosely inside! We still don't know how it got there and can't figure out who would've put it there. Maybe it was just supernatural! But it is amazing nonetheless how God provides again and again.

My Emotional Outlet

I have found that writing poetry and songs is great therapy for me. Writing has been a coping skill to help me with my emotions for as long as I can remember. It is much easier for me to write something out just the way I want it if I am trying to express my feelings, rather than just talking about them. I can make sure I say everything I want to say in writing and take out anything that I might decide doesn't sound quite right. It's a great way to not put my foot in my mouth and regret saying something that I can't take back.

Here are some of the poems and songs I have written over the years. Several were written while I was at the behavioral health center as an inpatient. Jeremy and I are hoping to someday record a CD of the songs, but I will put the lyrics in here.

Poems

You Never Brought Me Flowers

You never brought me flowers
When I was weak and trapped
I never got a single rose
When the door opened its flap
You came to visit, bringing smiles
And caring hearts a glow
You never brought me flowers
I just thought you should know.

(October, 1999)

Sometimes No Is the Best Answer

Some people tell us no
And it's for the best
Others tell us yes
And it hurts us in the end

What would you rather?
A safe no or a harmful yes?
God will never hurt us
He decides the true answers

Trust

Trust in God
He will give you an answer

It may not be the one you want to hear
But it will be for the best

So whatever situation you're in
Don't give up
And never, never give up on God
He will never leave you or forsake you

So never fear
God will be there
Holding your hand
Through the good and the bad

Maybe there is a lesson
Left here to be learned
Search your heart deep inside
God will show you the answer

(October, 1999)

My Trials

I am like Paul, singing in prison
But I understand why I'm here
To help myself and spread the Word
To those in this vast sphere

I am like Job, tempted by Satan
God has allowed these things to happen
All for a reason that's coming clear
One day I'll be free, I look forward to then

I am like Moses, pleading with Pharaoh
He keeps saying no, which was for the best
God hardened his heart and I didn't like it
His answer was no nevertheless

Perseverance is the key
To every situation in life
Now I see that if I'm strong
It makes me a better mother, daughter, wife

So through all this pain and suffering
I've found inner peace inside
For I believe God's still working on everyone
Now forever in Thee I'll abide

(October, 1999)

—⟊—

Morning Observances

Wind chimes sound the arrival of the breeze
As the branches dance around nearby trees
Water gently laps at the shore and dock below
The sun's reflection ripples, creating a diamond-
like glow
A morning at Westshore Drive
Helps a person feel rejuvenated, alive
My face feels the intermittent wind
A refreshing way to let the day begin

(June, 2004)

—⟊—

Make Each Day a Journey

What is the greatest challenge
That our lives have brought to view?
For some it could be a constant want
Of an ongoing desire or two

Instead of speeding everything up
Let's slow down and be content
With the situation we are in
Live for Jesus moment to moment

Through our journey, life may become
Dull, repetitive, maybe boring
It feels like we're stuck in a rut
When we should be eagles soaring

Instead of thinking, *It's time for a change*
A better thought instead
To make the best of where I am
To bloom where I'm planted

(September, 2005)

—⧓—

Praise of Thanks

Jesus, I thank You
For dying for me
Sinless You were
To set me free

Your blood was shed
A pardon for all
My life I give You
Never to fall

Please accept my
Effort of praise
I'll ever be true
All of my days

My heart I give
Freely to Thee
Openly living
For all to see

(September, 2006)

—m—

Feeling Down

What do I do?
I sometimes get depressed
My mind says
I just want to lie down
But if I listen
Things just don't get done
I have to get past
My feelings
And make myself
Do what needs to be done
This mood will pass
It always does
I'll feel myself again
Just don't give up

Down
Everlasting
Permeable
Reality
Enveloping
Sleep
Sad
Intruding
Oppressed
Negative

(October, 2006)

—m—

Trapped

Feeling like I'm trapped
Is worse than being alone
I feel like I don't want to do things
I feel like I'm a drone

A robot doing routine things
"No escape" my brain replays
Negative thoughts barge my mind
And fill up all my days

How to get out, how to escape
Scenes my mind plans out
Well-thought-out they are not
"I quit" is the constant shout

I'll never feel better
This will never be right

I'm overcommitted
I've lost the fight

"Give in! Give in!" To irrational actions
A war between two extremes
Positive and negative weighs in my mind
Between many, many screams

Will there ever be peace?
Will my mind be quiet again?
Only with God's help can I beat it
Only by prayer I can win

Saved!

I am saved!
No matter if I feel it
As long as I keep trying
Following His words

I am saved!
When things bother me
My mind is put at ease
Knowing someday it will be better

I am saved!
Blessed assurance
Trusting that Jesus's sacrifice
Is enough

I am saved!
My life shows it

How I live affirms it
My faith and beliefs

I am saved!
My past, my present, my future
All in His hands
He is at the wheel

I am saved!
Hearing, believing, repenting
Obeying His words
Baptized into Him
And raised anew

I am saved!
Life forever changed
Happiness uncontained
Waiting for eternity to begin

Freedom

I am saved!
No matter if I feel it
One day I might
Another day I don't feel it
But God is there
I know He'll never fail
He keeps His promises
And I believe Him
Ask Him
Seek Him
Knock and He will open doors

To wondrous things
To happiness beyond your dreams
To His love
And a life of blessings
If you will just let Him
Step into your heart
And allow the blood
To be the ticket
To your freedom

A Bedtime Prayer for Peace

Peace: a gentle feeling, focused,
Happy and content
The healing power of Jesus is
Clearly heaven-sent

When things start to get me down
Is when I choose to say
Prince of peace, please grant me sleep
For I know You are The Way

Journey to Sleep

Tension builds
My brain teases me
Anxiety for a moment
That moment past
Relaxation, a goal
My mind is set at ease
As I think of God's promises

And how He is faithful
My fears subside
Peace envelops me
I know He is near
A safe wall of angels
Watch over me as I dream
My thoughts put to rest
My body sleeps
Relaxation is achieved

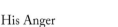

His Anger

Anger
A burning deep within
A roaring lion
Without restraint
The word *no*
Sends him in a spiral
A trigger
That creates a chain reaction
A different person comes out
Terrifying screams and shouts
There is no reasoning
No response when asked
Talking is out of the question
When the fire is lit
Respectfulness, thoughtfulness
Traits to be desired
Not present here
Anger

Assurance

Confidence in my salvation?
I feel like it's prideful
To really "know" where I am going
Seems a little too insightful

But what does God's Word say?
Am I basing faith on feelings?
When will I "get it" and have peace
Instead of bringing constant appeals?

A fear that at the end of life
That God will somehow say
"You missed one important thing
Sorry, no eternal day!"

It's not based on works
Or anything I can do
I know it in my heart
But in my head, do I believe it too?

So how do I conquer this?
These terrible feelings of fear?
To move toward true freedom?
To cry confident, yet humble tears?

To sin is not believing
God knows the best for me
It's when I'm not trusting
In His power to set me free

So putting behind my past
I'll press on toward the light
Instead of an occasional glimmer of hope
Be a candle shining bright

I'm not ashamed to tell others
How my faith has got me through
All of the terrible problems
That threw my mind askew

But if I can't get a grasp
On the truth of the Gospel
How can I share with others?
That's next to impossible

But I want my joy to be complete
To know deep in my soul
That He holds me and He keeps me
Until He calls the final roll

And on that day, my one defense
The only thing I can say
When He asks, *why should I let you in?*
Only because Jesus washed my sins away

(August, 2013)

—w—

Quiet Me

A gentle and quiet spirit
Lord, this I desire

I want to come before You
Listening as You inspire

Resting in Your presence
Is what my heart longs for
I knock and I am waiting
Please open up the door

As I humbly bow down
Coming to Your throne room
Amazed at Your holiness
Allow Your presence to consume

Father, One and Only
Great I AM forever
Let me not forget
Neither from You ever sever

Quiet my heart, O God
As I come to pray
Change me from within
Each and every day

(October, 2014)

—⚯—

The Battlefield of Prayer
(Ephesians 6:10–18)

Before we come to God in prayer
We first must realize
This is not a battle of the flesh
That we see with human eyes

In heavenly realms there is a fight
A spiritual war pursues
The devil and his army
Want their way to have you choose

But there's a way God gave us
To win the battle fierce
If we put His words in practice
The sword of the Spirit will always pierce

The armor of God prepares us
So we can stand our ground
The first thing holds the armor together
The truth of Jesus belted around

A breastplate of righteousness
Fits over heart and soul
Protecting us as we obey
As He keeps making us whole

We strap on our boots
Ready for our orders
To wherever God may lead us
Taking the Gospel to all borders

The shield of faith we hold in front
As we trust in God's protection
It foils Satan's plans to harm us
As we continue in self-reflection

The helmet we place upon our head
Is the assurance in our mind
Of the eternal salvation
That those who trust in Jesus find

At last we take up the sword
God's Word our only blade
Rightly cutting to the heart
Of those for who we've prayed

Our armor complete, we take our stand
But not how you'd expect
In strength we fall down to our knees
As our hearts to God connect

(November, 2014)

—m—

Songs

Blood-Stained Glasses

All my sin wears me down
How can I be free?
Every day again and again
Disappointing Thee
Why even try? I say once more
As I toss and turn
Oh Lord my God, I pray today You will help me learn

You see me through blood-stained glasses
Jesus Your Son stands before You pure and clean
All I have to offer is sin to mar my soul
Through Jesus's blood You see me whole

When I come to You
With humble contrite heart

I'm renewed, a new creation
Have a brand-new start
Every day I wake up and walk in Your grace
My thankfulness fills up
My heart's space

You see me through blood-stained glasses
Jesus Your Son stands before You pure and clean
All I have to offer is sin to mar my soul
Through Jesus's blood You see me whole

When I start to waiver
Getting lost in anxious thought
Remind me of Your Son who died
And salvation brought
When I start depending on me
Controlling my own life
Point me toward Jesus
Help me let go of my strife

You see me through blood-stained glasses
Jesus Your Son stands before You pure and clean
All I have to offer is sin to mar my soul
Through Jesus's blood You see me whole

Through Jesus's blood You see me whole

(2013)

—⟋⟍—

Like I See Jesus

Sitting in a room
You're there across from me
In my mind a vision
Of what You think of me

I want to hide myself from You
I don't live up to what You want me to

Let me see you, God
Like I see Jesus
Look upon your face
To see His smile
Father, when I look at Jesus
He's a reflection of You
So help me accept Your grace

Holy Father God
So good and perfect
How can You look at me
With love?

Why do I feel so condemned?
When I know what You've done for me.

Let me see You, God
Like I see Jesus
Look upon Your face
To see His smile
Father, when I look at Jesus
He's a reflection of You
So help me accept Your grace

I somehow separate
You Father, from Your Son.
Jesus's arms accept me
Sayin' we've already won

But, God, I see You with a frown
Thinking how I'm disappointing You

Let me see you, God
Like I see Jesus
Look upon Your face
To see His smile
Father, when I look at Jesus
He's a reflection of You
So help me accept Your grace

I decide to believe
Your ways are not my own
Part of faith is trusting
I can't do it all alone

Please be patient as I learn
Just how much You've always loved me

Now I see You, God
Like I see Jesus
I look upon Your face
And see You smile
Father, when I look at Jesus
He's a reflection of You
So I accept Your grace

(2014)

Come Back

Pain
Deep inside
Hurting
I'm wondering why
I feel for you
But I can't understand
Why you keep it all inside
And you say you're happy

But
I know you're hurting inside
Remember
God will never let you go
He never left you
You can come back to Him
His arms are wide open for you

You don't have to do this alone
I know someone that you need
He loves you right where you are
So come back to His arms again

Years
It's been years
Never reaching out
Never asking for help
I can do this on my own
No one will understand me

But you never gave us a chance to
Help you

Why
Why do you fight it?
Defending
Justifying yourself
When you know deep inside
What is really true
Please oh please don't deny it anymore

You don't have to do this alone
I know someone that you need
He loves you right where you are
So come back to Him arms again

He's
There waiting for you
Why do you
Hesitate
He can heal the years of pain
That you've kept locked away
Don't hide anymore
He wants your heart again

My
Heart hurts for you
But God
He hurts even more
Your heart is what He wants
The only way you'll be happy
Is to fill the void
With Him

You don't have to do this alone
I know someone that you need
He loves you right where you are
So come back to His arms again

(2014)

—◆—

Perfect

Growing up I thought I had to be perfect
Dotting my i's and crossing my t's
Always striving to do better
I was my own worst enemy

I brought this into my relationship with You
Now I'm trying to undo
The years of lies I've told myself

Now I'm learning
To accept who I am
And I don't have to be perfect
You died for me
And I'm clothed in You
Jesus, You've made me perfect

This doesn't mean I don't give any effort
So grace can just cover me
It's the *why* behind the action
Not to earn the approval from You

It's black or white, all or nothing with me
There's no balance in my life
I'm putting faith in myself

Now I'm learning
To accept who I am
And I don't have to be perfect
You died for me
And I'm clothed in You
Jesus You've made me perfect

Help us all to see
The power's not in us
There is nothing we can do
To get ourselves back to You

You can learn
To accept who you are
You don't have to be perfect
He died for you
And you're clothed in Him
Jesus makes you perfect

By trusting what You did for us
Jesus, You are perfect
So we don't have to be

(2014)

—ɯ—

Let Go

Bring me to my knees
To surrender once more
Let Your grace cover me
Like never before

Until I understand
How sinful I am
I can't appreciate
Your love

You died on the cross
A perfect sacrifice
Only once for all my sin
So why should I bring it up again

So let go, let go
You set me free
Let go, let go
When You died for me
Let go, let go
Press on to the prize
Let go, let go
How wonderful someday
To be by Your side

I want to show love
To all the people
On the earth that You
Died for

How can I live
Silently when the good news is
Alive in me

I'll sing to tell
The world Your love
So everyone can know
And praise You

So let go, let go
You set me free
Let go, let go
When You died for me
Let go, let go
Press on to the prize
Let go, let go
How wonderful someday
To be by Your side

(2014)

—∿—

Lord of My Life

Be Lord of my life
To only You be true
Keep my loyalty
Solely just for You

When my sinfulness
Pierces through and through
Change my heart O God
Which only You can do

Lead me deeper
Deeper
Deeper in Your grace
Wash me whiter
Whiter
Whiter than snow

Temptation beckons me
But You help me to
Deny myself
When I struggle to

Father, take me now
Make me more like You
Mold me with your hands
That I surrender to

Lead me deeper
Deeper
Deeper In Your grace
Wash me whiter
Whiter
Whiter than snow

Be Lord of my life
To only You be true
Keep my loyalty
Solely just for You

(2014)

—◊◊—

Arms of Jesus

When I heard a voice
That sounded like you calling
My heart immediately sprang to life

With excitement and joy
'Til I heard it wasn't your voice
I felt my soul sink deep

Fall into the arms of Jesus
Fall into the arms of grace
Fall into redemption
Oh, what a wonderful place

Don't give into despair
I need Your Holy Spirit
To breathe life into my soul

You're holding me
And you understand my hurting
With tears of perfect peace

Fall into the arms of Jesus
Fall into the arms of grace
Fall into redemption
Oh, what a wonderful place

He sings over me
And into my spirit
Telling me, *Be strong, hold on*

You're with me all the way
And You're melting all the pain
So I can live for You

Fall into the arms of Jesus
Fall into the arms of grace
Fall into redemption
Oh, what a wonderful place

Your love will never leave
You constantly remind me
You're my eternal friend

And when I start to slip
Away into the darkness
You strengthen me again

Fall into the arms of Jesus
Fall into the arms of grace
Fall into redemption
Oh, what a wonderful place

Lyrics by Kayla Warner and Ginger Kelley
Music by Jeremy Warner

(2014)

Kayla and Jeremy on their wedding day, February 14, 1998

Levi's "chocolate milk" experiment

Chocolate footprints down the hall

"I'm having a chocolate bath!"

Children from the Indian orphan home we support

Special way of honoring us after the Ladies
Conference in India, January 2014

Arrival to India greeting December 2013

The Warner family, Jeremy, Kayla,
Levi and Miles, December 2014